Dedicated to the world and everyone in it.

LUCIFER EVE AND ADAM

THE ABSOLUTELY TRUE AND COMPLETELY HONEST STORY OF CREATION.

PETER WILKES and
CATHERINE DICKEY WILSON

with a little help from Mark Twain

Published by Lakehurst Publishing

ISBN-13: 978-0998239705
ISBN-10: 0998239704

Illustrations by Catherine Dickey Wilson
Cover Design by Dane Low @creativeindiecovers.com
Layout by Guido Henkel

Printed in the U.S.A.

LUCIFER EVE AND ADAM

THE WHYS
AND THE WHEREFORES

Now, I have no idea if this is true, but I've been told since I was a baby that Mark Twain was my cousin… twice removed on my mother's side… by way of her half-cousin on her stepsister's side… the stepsister, of course, being the bastard child of one *Seymour* Clemens who was said to be the direct descendent of Samuel Clemens… that is, his fifth cousin three times removed on his father's side.

Anyway—in spite of the impeccable sources of that information passed down through the generations—I never felt particularly inspired to further investigate Mark Twain's life or delve into the relationship. So that's why, I suppose, Mark decided to come visit *me* about a year ago.

At least his voice did… which, when you're as old as I am, can be a somewhat suspect event. But, I knew right away it was the voice of the real Mark Twain, because he sounded exactly like Hal Holbrook.

Now, I did, as a kid—with him being related and all— read a bunch of his books, and one was called *Eve's Diary*. It was about what actually happened in The Garden of Eden. You knew it was genuine because Mr.

Twain was translating directly from the authentic diary which he had found someplace in Africa. The story was brilliant... as far as it went. You see, there were gaps. Mr. Twain explained that since the diary was old, a lot of it had crumbled away, therefore it made sense that parts of it would be missing.

So, all these years that particular story has been sitting in the back of my mind. But, lately, it's kind of moved to the front because of the world being in the state it's in. I mean, after all, Eve and Adam *were* the original source of humanity, so it seems logical that if we better understood what actually happened at the <u>beginning</u> of time, then we might understand what we need to do to get out of the mess we find ourselves in <u>today</u>.

And I was thinking those very same thoughts when that voice of Mark Twain came into my ear. And he says to me, "Peter, you're my first cousin, twice removed, on your mother's side... by way of her half-cousin..." and he went through the entire litany before he finally came to the punch line.

"You're blood. You're kin. You've got to finish it."

"Finish what?" I asked.

"The diary. Eve's diary. You've need to fill in the gaps. You have to tell the rest of the story."

"Uh... How in the world?—"

"You can't *in* the world. See, I'm not there. I'm up here. With her."

"Eve? You're with Eve?" Instinctively, I looked up. To my great relief all I saw was my ceiling.

"Well, she's here too, but I mean the *real* her."

Panic hit. Discussions—serious or otherwise—with disembodied voices was not on my bucket list.

"I'm here with The Creator," Mark forged ahead, "The Creator of the Universe. God, Yahweh, Allah, Krishna, whatever you want to call her. And she's gonna"—

"Wait. The Creator's a she?" Was this what the onset of Alzheimer's looked like?

"Well, you can't really see her. It's like she's… every-*where* and every*thing*. But the Voice of The Creator is most definitely female."

And it most definitely was.

"Hi, Peter." Damn, now *two* voices in my head?! This new voice, however, was distinctly different from Mark's. Proud, all knowing, it was also soft and gentle and kind. Had I literally met my maker?… Omigod, was I?—

"No," the voice was soothing, "you're not dead. Not yet. I have a job for you."

Now, except for weddings and funerals I hadn't darkened the door of a house of worship for fifty-seven years, so I hardly felt prepared for what followed.

"As Mark – that is, your cousin Samuel – has implied," The Creator continued, "I want to tell you the real and honest story of <u>Eve</u> and Adam and, once I do, I'd like *you* to relay it to humankind."

"W…Why me?" I was floored.

"Because you unfortunately absorbed—like a sponge—the current version of <u>Adam</u> and Eve at a very young age."

"Didn't everybody?"

"But it made <u>you</u> feel special." She was right about that. My dad was a minister and, above all, preacher's kids had to be the smartest in Sunday School. And since Sunday School seemed to be the only place I <u>could</u> feel smart, I imprinted every one of those bible stories on my young brain.

"What you absorbed was… misguided." With a noted testiness on that last word, The Creator went on. "In the first place it wasn't *Adam* and Eve, it was *Eve* and Adam. While the two were equal in every sense of the word, Eve should have always had the slightly higher billing, as you will soon see. So, be sure and use your wife as you write this story. You're going to need feminine input, big time. However, above and beyond all that, it's most important to understand the real story was Lucifer. For every good reason known to *him*, he had withheld love from the human race, and needed to be taught a lesson…"

"Oh, one more thing. Write it like a movie script so Hollywood will buy it. We need wide distribution on this story."

"Hollywood'll never buy this one," I heard cousin Samuel sigh. "Eve and Adam's nudity will never make it past the censor board."

"Well, it's high time for the censor board to rethink their priorities," The Creator snipped. "It <u>was</u> the Garden of Eden, the weather was perfect, and clothes weren't invented!! Plus, it's the original love story—brilliant, fun, and very real. What more could a producer possibly want?... Shall we begin?"

Now, I know enough about writing to say that if Mark Twain offers you suggestions, it's probably wise to heed them.

And, if you're past a certain age and hearing The Creator's voice, I believe you damn well better do what *she* suggests. So I got some writing stuff and spent the next several weeks taking copious notes.

After she said "the end" and we said goodbye I never heard from the two of them again, so I'm guessing my wife Dickey and I got most of the story right. And for my money, this version makes a heck of a lot more sense—especially these days—than the one certain folks have been telling us for thousands and thousands of years.

But then it's probably best if you judge that for yourself...

MAP OF PARADISE
by EVE
Moon
Moonview Plateau
Waterfall
Lion's Den
Waterfall Pool
Paradise Mountain
Adam's Cave
Vegetable Patch
Adam's Lake
Paradise Meadow
My Pond
My Forest
Adam's Forest
2437 STEPS
----- Paths

Lucifer Eve and Adam

CAST OF CHARACTERS

Lucifer – an immaculately dressed angel, ageless, wingless, whose understanding of humanity has been forever clouded by his fear of love.

Eve – an average woman, early 20's, practical, feisty and—being the first woman on earth—totally in the dark about men.

Adam – an average guy, early 20's, head-strong, impulsive and—being the first man on earth—totally in the dark about women.

The Creator – The Creator's age is understandably indeterminate. In form, the resemblance is human. In dress, there's sweatpants and a t-shirt with THE CREATOR on the front for identification. And that's a good thing because, in looks, The Creator is forever morphing and changing: combining genders, ages, races and forms of every living thing that has ever graced the face of this earth. It's important you remember this going forward.

But in voice? In voice there's no question that The Creator is female. Thus we will use the pronoun "she" for the duration.

LUCIFER EVE AND ADAM

CHAPTER 1

Darkness… All other thoughts fade as a distant scene appears in the mind's eye…

The scene is clearer now. We're in deep, deep outer space. Meteors, comets, asteroids ZIP by as stars EX-PLODE all around a—

1940's airplane?

Yes. Oddly, a 1947 Spruce Goose—300-foot wingspan, eight huge, whirling propellers—is adeptly dodging the fiery meteors and asteroids when, from inside the aircraft, we hear a—

> **Panicked male voice:** Wha… Wha… What in _your_ name _is_ this thing?!

> **Female voice:** _(irritated)_ An airplane. It hasn't been invented yet…

Inside the Spruce Goose the female voice—and the PILOT—is **THE CREATOR**. Dressed for work in her t-shirt and sweat pants, she glares at the panicky angel in the seat beside her.

Meet **LUCIFER**—sartorially resplendent in white tie and tails—whose terror of this crazy airplane contraption grows by the nanosecond.

> **Lucifer:** Please, you've gotta believe… I wasn't trying to—

> **Creator:** Forget what you were trying or not trying to do. Look at what's happening now!

Furious, The Creator points to a 1950's black-and-white TV duct-taped to the control panel. On the screen is—

The Garden of Eden—softness… and light… a wondrous flower-filled meadow surrounded by a lush, primordial forest. In the near distance, the early afternoon sun reflects off a waterfall flowing over the side of a small and gorgeous mountain.

Pairs of creatures, bathed in the warm sunlight, are everywhere. Pairs of elephants trundle across the meadow, trunks entwined. Overhead, the gander and goose trumpet happily to one another. As pairs of butterflies flutter over wavy grasses, the mare and stallion, ewe and ram, doe and buck all peacefully share the expanse with the lioness and lion, tigress and tiger. It's contentment, harmony, and happiness all around…

Except with one particular pair—**EVE** and **ADAM**—who, eyes blazing, are in middle of an argument in the middle of the VEGETABLE PATCH at the foot of PARADISE MOUNTAIN.

> **Adam:** What?! Why not?!!

Adam is totally flabbergasted by the only woman in the world he has ever seen.

Eve: I said I don't see the point.

Both Eve and Adam are naked (of course), and Adam has a huge erection.

Adam: Whatta you mean you don't see the point?

He jabs his finger at his crotch.

Adam: It's right there.

Eve: Not that point, the other point.

That confuses Adam even more.

Eve: The point of why you think you are needed…

Eve holds up a cucumber she's picked from a nearby vine.

Eve: … when I've found a perfectly adequate replacement?

Adam: But… but…

He points to <u>each</u> of their crotches.

Adam: <u>This</u> sees <u>that</u> and they do it.

Eve: They <u>can</u> do it, but like I said—

Adam: You saw <u>my</u> point before!

Back in the Spruce Goose, The Creator scowls at Lucifer.

Creator: Does that sound like they're seeing the true beauty in each other?

Lucifer: I'm sure it's just a matter of adjust-ment—

Creator: Do they appear to be rejoicing in each other's differences as we discussed on numerous occasions?

Lucifer: Some fine tuning, perhaps—

Creator: Fine tuning?! They're a mess. And they're a mess because <u>you</u> didn't stick to the original plan. The basic ingredient isn't there!

Down in the vegetables, Eve and Adam are still at it.

Eve: Look, when we did it before, something was missing.

Adam: Not for me.

Eve: Yep. I understand that part.

Adam: So what, then?

Eve: *(hesitantly)* That's the part I don't un-derstand.

Adam's totally… deflated. They both eye his crotch.

Eve: Whew. Least it's going down.

Adam: I think I set a new record.

Eve: Okay. About that. Why are you doing it with… everything?

Adam: This is Paradise! How are you not getting that?

Eve: It just seems like a lot.

Adam: I do it with everything in Paradise because everything in Paradise is put here to do it with!… At least <u>most</u> everything.

That last comment—directed at Eve—is ignored.

Eve: For example?

Adam: Well, if I could catch them, the sheep and goats would be…

"Perfect" is the word Adam's searching for, but since he doesn't know that word, he has to act it out.

Adam: On the other hand the rocks, which <u>don't</u> move…

Are kinda blah.

Adam: The rose bush, the alligator…

Ouch!

Adam: Sun-warmed cantaloupes, however…

He grabs one from a vine. They're the best!

Adam: Cantaloupes…

Are WOW!

Eve ponders this demonstration, shrugs.

Eve: I think I'm gonna stick with my cucumber.

Adam: Why?

Eve: I dunno. One seems enough.

In the Spruce Goose, The Creator's almost speechless. Lucifer squirms under her critical eye.

Creator: They don't even know the words.

Lucifer: They know <u>some</u> words—

Creator: They feel things they can't express. And what about nuance! This complete failure to communicate is because <u>what</u>, exactly, is missing?!

Lucifer: *(miserable)* L... l... love.

Creator: Why, Lou? Why'd you do it? Tell me why you left it out.

Lucifer: Because if they know what love <u>is</u>, then they'd also have to know what love <u>is</u> <u>not</u>. They'd have to know hate... and neglect...

As Lucifer talks it's clear these words are profoundly painful for him.

Lucifer: ... disloyalty, misery, sorrow, and... *(almost in tears)* ... the worst of all— indifference.

Lucifer is doing his best to conceal his pain from the all-seeing, all-knowing, Creator—obviously a futile task—and she softens at his effort. Her beloved angel has always been a late bloomer...

But now we're down to crunch time and—having the hardest head of any angel in the universe—he is a long way from figuring <u>any</u> of this out.

As evidence: Lucifer—quickly masking his misery—immediately returns to business.

Lucifer: Therefore, as I am, by your decree, in <u>charge</u> of Love and Human Happiness—an astute choice on your part I might add…

The Creator silently scoffs. And why do you think I made that choice?

Lucifer: … I have come to the conclusion that humans don't need love to find happiness and that therefore love, with its attendant downside, will not be finding its way into Paradise.

This is unbelievable. There was so much wrong with that statement, there's only one place to start. The freaking beginning.

Creator: Again, you left the "Love and Human Happiness" class early.

Lucifer: There are 767 trillion, 832 million, 698 thousand, 141 <u>other</u> angels in that class. It is impossible for you to know whether I was there or—

Creator: Did you just hear yourself? Have you learned nothing?! And your number's wrong. The angel count is 140, not 141. Azazel was placed on personal leave.

Lucifer: *(aghast)* Why?

Creator: Because his <u>personal</u> issues were impeding the work.

Lucifer: Well, I'm sorry to hear that.

However, The Creator's comment has disarmed Lucifer. He unconsciously pats his immaculate tailcoat, reassuring himself of the contents of an inner pocket.

The Creator, of course, doesn't miss this either. Wow. Really? _Total_ denial, Lou? She sighs. Okay then, we're doing this the hard way.

WHAM-WHAM-WHAM! Something outside slams again and again into the Spruce Goose causing Lucifer's angelic life to flash before his eyes!

> **Lucifer:** *(terror)* Help, no, wait! I'm in this all the way with these two. You _do_ know that, right?!

> **Creator:** Yes, Lou. I certainly do know that. Quite well, actually.

WHAM-WHAM-WHAM! The Creator pays the disturbance no mind.

> **Lucifer:** *(fearful penance)* Yes, yes, okay. I did leave class a bit early.

The **WHAMMING** stops.

> **Lucifer:** I needed to make a few adjustments on our humans. We _were_ under a deadline.

> **Creator:** Yeah, well those adjustments now mean that those two humans are never getting together. So, here's a news flash! In order for any _human_ plan to work, there's got to be a _human_ race to begin with. And that does not seem to be happening!!

Which is becoming abundantly clear because Adam—with <u>three</u> cantaloupes under his arms—has now had it with Eve.

Adam: I'm leaving. A cantaloupe calls.

Instinctively he nods politely to Eve… wonders why he did that… and heads toward <u>his</u> forest that borders the east side of PARADISE MEADOW.

As he departs, Eve—instinctively—eyes his oh-so-attractive butt.

> **Eve:** *(after him)* Maybe someday you could be <u>better</u> than a cucumber.
>
> **Adam:** *(without stopping)* I have no idea what "better" means.
>
> **Eve:** I don't either, but it seems to go together with "worse," another new word which just came to me. I need to think about them.
>
> **Adam:** You think too much.

He grumbles into the forest. Eve shrugs.

> **Eve:** I'll be around if you wanna talk.
>
> **Adam:** What's "talk?"
>
> **Eve:** I already told you. It's what we did the other day before you jumped me, and what we just did.
>
> **Adam:** Don't like "talk." Makes me lose focus.

Eve shrugs and heads toward <u>her</u> forest on the west side of Paradise Meadow.

In the plane, Lucifer shrivels under The Creator's glare.

> **Lucifer:** *(covering)* Okay. The major issue could be that the superior communication function in the female—

> **Creator:** Led to an overload of hormones in the male? That makes no sense!

> **Lucifer:** We're exploring the possible causes now, but the pair did do it once—

> **Creator:** Listen to you. "The pair?" What are they to you, just… operating systems?

> **Lucifer:** Very efficient operating systems—

> **Creator:** Well, not efficient enough, because the "pairing" of that "pair" didn't take!

> **Lucifer:** It didn't? Huh? That wasn't supposed to happen. Well, then, the problem must be—

> **Creator:** Yours, Lucifer, to solve. I have the entire rest of the universe to deal with today.

> **Lucifer:** Which I <u>will</u> solve—

> **Creator:** In eleven hours and eleven minutes.

She points at a DIGITAL CLOCK, also duct-taped to the control panel, displaying **11:11** in BIG numbers.

> **Lucifer:** What?! Eleven?—

Creator: The perfect time of alignment where—hopefully for you—everything will be exactly where it needs to be.

Lucifer: A riddle? Really, at a time like this?

Creator: *(ignoring him)* From the moment you hit the earth's atmosphere—

Lucifer: What?! I'm going to earth?

Creator: From the moment you hit the earth's atmosphere you will have one hour, forty-three minutes and thirty seconds of daylight today, six hours and twenty-eight minutes of darkness tonight, and two hours, fifty-nine minutes and thirty seconds after sunrise tomorrow—

Lucifer: No… no way! It just can't happen that fast!

WHAM! The Creator yanks the plane into a DIVE throwing Lucifer into a brand new panic.

Lucifer: B… b… better idea. Why don't we give things time to work themselves out, and we get out of this crazy airplane—

Creator: You just don't get it, do you!

Lucifer: Of course I do, I invented time. At least daytime…

The Creator rolls her eyes. Lucifer's appropriately chagrined.

Lucifer: Okay, well maybe not daytime, but I invented <u>telling</u> time by looking at the sun. That counts for something.

Creator: And yet you gave no thought to the moon, or the tides, or to all the other living, breathing cycles of the earth?!

Lucifer: I gave… some thought. A little.

Creator: But none, apparently, to the part that says Eve is fertile only until eight-thirty-two tomorrow morning!

Lucifer: What?!

Creator: If these two don't do it by then—given their cucumbers and cantaloupes and whatever else—not only won't they be speaking in twenty-eight days, they'll be on opposite sides of their world! Humankind will never exist!!

She sighs, shakes her head.

Creator: You cut <u>how</u> many classes?

CHAPTER 2

Shadowed by pairs of silent creatures, Adam grumbles to himself as he trudges to his cave a short distance up Paradise Mountain.

> **Adam:** It makes no sense. In Paradise you get what you want. So, if I <u>want</u> to do it with her, how come she doesn't <u>want</u> to do it with me?

But, on Eve's side of Paradise, the creatures are cheered by the sound of her voice.

> **Eve:** I can't keep re-figuring things! I had just gotten used to it being me alone here in Paradise with *(to the woods)* all of you…

Pairs of birds and butterflies respond with cheerful fluttering.

> **Eve:** Even <u>with</u> the one hitch which, for a place called Paradise, didn't seem as it should…

That gets the attention of all the creatures.

> **Eve:** See… you all seem to understand <u>me</u> when I talk to <u>you</u>, but I can't seem to under-stand <u>you</u> when you talk to <u>me</u>. At least, not exactly. Not exactly like this new creature

and I understand each other. And I think it's going to be important to be exactly understood in this world…

An understanding sigh from the flora and fauna.

Eve: Now, what role this new creature has to play in all that, I don't know. It seems like I've been put on this earth to say words, to name things, and to talk about them so everything somehow makes sense. But it seems like he's been put on this earth to do his thing with cantaloupes and the like. It doesn't feel like these two go together at all, but… In the meantime, all these words that I need to introduce to the world are firing into my brain. Which is okay when they come with an obvious meaning, like "cow" and "tree." But some, like this new one, "lonely?"…

Tree branches dip in empathy as the animals surround her in comfort.

Eve: I don't have a clue what that means. It's all becoming a bit overwhelming.

But, for Adam, now in his **MAN-CAVE**, nothing's overwhelming. In fact, it's all quite straightforward.

Sunlight beams through an opening in the cave's ceiling directly onto Adam's crude drawings on the wall. These are his "centerfolds." He examines each one closely, etches yet <u>another</u> big check mark next to the cantaloupe with his writing rock…

…casts a wistful glance at the sheep and the goat…

...comes to the gazelle...

Adam: *(sad sigh)* Couldn't catch that one either.

The rose bush and crocodile have big **"X's"** through them, which Adam <u>re</u>emphasizes...

And that brings him to his newest drawing—that of Eve...

Adam: So, whatta you think, Horton?

Adam turns to a **ROCK**—the size of a small watermelon—on which he has crudely drawn a face. This is **HORTON**. Adam listens for a moment, then nods in agreement. He turns back to his drawing of Eve and puts a big **X** through her as well.

Satisfied, he sits down, drapes his arm over the rock. Horton's his buddy.

Adam: *(to Horton)* You know, you're the only creature I've found I can really talk to—

Adam—seemingly interrupted—suddenly listens carefully to Horton, grins, then gives the rock a whole-hearted "slap on the back."

Adam: You always know <u>exactly</u> what I want.

Grabbing a cantaloupe from his ample supply, he gives it a sexy, knowing look and deftly slices the end off with his writing rock.

Up in the Spruce Goose, The Creator shakes her head in disbelief. Lucifer attempts to anticipate her question.

Lucifer: So, yes—for the moment—man's best friend is a rock. The dog is on its way. Just need to work out a few kinks.

Creator: This is about <u>them</u>, Lou! You've completely missed the grand plan.

Lucifer: What grand plan?

Creator: I rest my case.

The Creator's voice is testy but there's compassion in her eyes, a compassion that says, "Every soul needs to find its own way."

But all Lucifer sees is problem after problem with no way out…

And zero help from his now silent boss.

One of Eve's favorite places in Paradise is a quiet pond in a small clearing in the exact center of her forest. And that's where we find her, staring with a furrowed brow at her reflection in the still water.

Eve: I believe I am a plan that is grand, although I don't know what that means…

Pairs of forest creatures watch quietly as she absently tosses a twig into the water.

Eve: But if <u>I'm</u> a grand plan, then what is the <u>new</u> creature?

She sighs as she watches the twig float away, pushed by a casual current.

> **Eve:** And how is someone, who's only two weeks old, supposed to figure <u>that</u> out, too?

Her eyes suddenly darken.

> **Eve:** Uh, oh. "Two," "to," and "too" in one sentence. What does that mean?

And—twenty minutes later—Eve is <u>still</u> trying to figure things out as she follows a scowling Adam through Paradise Meadow.

> **Eve:** … so, last night I realized the stars are not organized. I tried moving them around with a stick to line them up in a row, but they were just out of reach.

> **Adam:** I could reach 'em.

> **Eve:** Could not.

> **Adam:** Could so. I could jump up.

Eve eyes the taller Adam. He may have a point… an intelligent one this time… so she changes the subject.

> **Eve:** Where was I? Right, the moon. That's the name I gave the big round star that's bigger than all the others. *(romantic sigh)* The moon is just so… something. I don't have the right word yet.

> **Adam:** *(under his breath)* <u>There's</u> a first.

> **Eve:** *(not hearing him)* But it'll come… Do you think the moon belongs to us?…

Eve's suddenly concerned.

> **Eve:** Oh my. What if it were someone else's and they took it back?…

Adam's scowl deepens as he picks up the pace… Eve, trailing, matches him stride for stride.

> **Eve:** I've got it! Moons are pretty and romantic. That's why I love 'em!

That's it. Adam quickly searches for the nearest tree. There! At the border of his forest. He races for it… leaps up on a low branch and climbs.

Eve, on his heels, grabs for the same limb, but can't reach it… so all she can do is glare up at him.

> **Eve:** Alright, what's this all about?

> **Adam:** I have no idea what the words "pretty," "romantic," and "love" mean, but they all—especially the last one—made me really <u>not</u> want to be with you.

> **Eve:** I don't understand them, either. Words just come into my head! But, if you and I talk about 'em, maybe we can figure 'em out.

> **Adam:** Told you. Don't like to talk.

> **Eve:** *(amazed)* How could you not like to talk?!

Adam climbs higher… again, that butt.

> **Eve:** Alright. If you're gonna be that way…

Pissed, Eve plops herself on a nearby patch of grass… a moment passes… and another…

Ohhh, he's just sooooo frustrating!…

Eve: If you're not gonna talk, I'm leaving.

She jumps back up.

Adam: I'll talk about numbers.

Eve: What are they?

Adam: One… Two…

Adam makes a suggestive gesture—which he does each time he says "one two." Eve gives him a final scowl and flounces away.

CHAPTER 3

As the Spruce Goose continues to speed through the galaxy, Lucifer's panic shifts from the airplane contraption to what to do about Eve and Adam. He glances again at the digital clock: still holding at 11:11.

Lucifer: That's really all the time I'll have?

Creator: From the moment you get there, yes.

Lucifer: *(indicating the plane)* Can't you make this thing go faster?

Creator: Nope.

Lucifer: Why not?

Creator: Because there's a time for every purpose—

Lucifer: Under heaven. Yes, I know. Why do you always speak in riddles?

Creator: Why do you never listen?

Lucifer: I do listen... I... *(distressed)* You know I would never hurt those two. You know that, right?

Ah! There it is, The Creator silently notes. He couldn't keep that buried forever. Lucifer does love Eve and Adam. But he can't acknowledge it. He can't he let them love him back.

> **Lucifer:** Look, all I was doing was—

> **Creator:** Tinkering. So that Eve and Adam could exist in life but never experience it.

But Lucifer—obsessing over his Eve and Adam dilemma—hears none of that last comment. As such, her point proven, all The Creator can do is shake her head in dismay.

On earth, Adam—now down from the tree—has waded, waist deep, into a nearby shallow lake and is making an unsuccessful attempt to catch little fish with his bare hands.

Eve—far too curious about Adam to have actually left—now spies on him from behind a bush.

> **Eve:** *(calls out)* So, your name is Adam. It just came to me…

Adam scowls at the sound of her voice and continues "fishing." That, in turn, causes Eve to return the scowl, leave her hiding place, and nonchalantly walk to the lake's edge.

> **Eve:** I'm Eve.

Adam couldn't care less.

Eve: Look, talking's important. And I <u>am</u> interesting so, clearly, if I can talk to another who can talk back to me, I'll be twice as interesting!

Adam: *(grins)* Twice? As in one, two?

That suggestive gesture again.

Eve: Don't you ever think about anything else?!

Adam: *(missing a fish)* Occasionally.

Eve: *(changing the subject)* Why are you trying to catch those things?

Adam: It's not like they come when they're called.

Eve: They're called fish.

Adam: Well, "fish" make me feel something…

Adam momentarily stops his fishing and softly touches his heart.

Adam: … in here.

Eve: Why?

Adam: *(back to fishing)* They're always under water. I tried being under water, and I couldn't breathe. So now when I think of them not breathing, it hurts me in that place. Then I saw they actually had little wavy legs on their sides so I thought I'd catch 'em and put them on land so they <u>could</u> breathe.

Then their little legs would grow, and they'd learn to walk.

Eve: *(thrilled)* You <u>do</u> like to talk.

Adam: Do not.

Eve: You just did.

Adam: That was a scientific observation. It's different.

Eve: Well, I don't think your scientific observation is right.

Adam: Why not?

Eve: I don't know.

Adam: I do. It's 'cause you didn't think of it yourself.

Adam wends his way back to dry land.

Eve: That's not true. It's just... I seem to be the gatherer of words.

Adam: Well, guess what? You may be the gatherer of words, but *(proudly)* I'm a plan that's grand!

Eve: Really? Do you know what that means? 'Cause I don't.

Adam: No. But I knew it the moment I arrived.

Eve: *(delighted)* So did I. I'm a plan that's grand too!

Adam: You are not.

Eve: Yes I am.

Adam: No. You're not.

Eve: I am, too.

Adam: Not.

Eve: Too.

Adam: Not!

Eve: Too!

Adam: No, we're different! I have wants!!

Eve: I have needs!

Adam: What are they?

Eve: I don't know.

Adam: There! That's absolute scientific proof we are <u>not</u> the same!!

In each other's faces, eyes blazing, the chemistry is intense...

...which causes such confusion the only thing to do...

...is to run away from each other as fast as humanly possible!

And, back in the plane, the only thing Lucifer can do after watching this little episode is to hem and haw.

Lucifer: Right... Okay... Confession time. Here's the problem. I can't implement the "love" program in time. It can't be done. It's just too complicated.

> **Creator:** Ever think you might be the one who is complicating it, Lou?

> **Lucifer:** I'm being practical. Love isn't critical for procreation: it just clouds everything up. You'll see. In fact, you'll thank me.

The Creator shakes her head, retreats into silence. Whatever you say, Lou. It's your journey…

> **Lucifer:** *(breaking the silence)* Look, I <u>will</u> fix this… In <u>eleven hours and eleven minutes</u> I will fix this… These two?… Like rabbits… You just wait.

But, my friend, you're going to have to take your journey more seriously.

> **Creator:** You know, Lou, we may have to rethink your role in this whole thing.

> **Lucifer:** What?! No, no, no, wait. That's like saying I'm <u>beyond</u> all hope. *(panic)* You never say that. You never say "<u>beyond</u> all" unless…

More silence from The Creator… and now it's deafening.

> **Lucifer:** That's not really possible, is it? That I could no longer be a part of <u>your</u> team? *(aghast)* That I, me, Lucifer, could be put on harp duty?…

Again, no answer.

> **Lucifer:** *(horror)* Or… or… be put on… "personal leave?" *(dread)* Or <u>never</u> get my angel wings?!?

Dead silence… except for the steady drone of the plane's engines bringing them closer and closer to a world that Lucifer does not understand. A shiver runs down his spine. This is serious. He better not—no, he <u>cannot</u>—fail.

CHAPTER 4

At the very same time, Eve—deep in thought—is wandering by herself across Paradise Meadow.

> **Eve:** It's called a man. And since I'm a woman, it sounds like there should be a connection. Like I'm the whole thing and he's a part of me, though what part, I have no idea. I don't seem to be missing anything. At least not anything that matters…

Her eyes are drawn to a day-old **LAMB** nuzzling its mother.

> **Eve:** Oh, what an adorable little… What is it?

Rushing over, she strokes the soft wool as the lamb frolics around her feet. Mama **EWE** looks on approvingly.

> **Eve:** It feels so… I don't have the word… *(to the Mama)* Where did you get this creature?

> **Mama EWE**: Baaaaaaa.

> **Eve:** I bet it came right out of the ground just like everything else, right? Well, that's

amazing, because it looks exactly like a teeny-tiny you.

Mama EWE: *(agreeing)* Baaaaaaa.

Eve: Maybe someday I can find one growing somewhere that looks like a teeny-tiny me.

But that's looking more and more impossible as, back in his man-cave, Adam grumbles to his silent buddy, Horton.

Adam: … it's that talk, talk, chatter, chatter, chatter noise that's driving me nuts. So what should I do? *(listens to Horton)* You're right. Noises—just like that thunder one we heard—should <u>always</u> be far away, so they sound soft and peaceful and quiet… *(IDEA!)* Of course. <u>Her</u> noise should be far away. So the solution is that <u>she</u> should always be far away. Alright, Horton, well done! *(he low-fives the rock)* And, now that we've taken care of that…

He grabs Horton from the ground.

Adam: It's time to get back to the real stuff.

Tucking the rock under his arm, Adam proudly tromps out of the cave. He and Horton have a <u>new</u> mission in life.

The late afternoon sun glows over Paradise Meadow as a male LION—mouth wide open—endures a dental exam by Eve. The LIONESS sits patiently by.

> **Eve:** I don't get it. Those are some kinda teeth…

Eve pulls on one tooth, taps on another, wiggles a third.

> **Eve:** You'd think they'd have a greater use than simply chomping on strawberries and peaches.

The Lion's stomach growls. Eve stops the examination.

> **Eve:** You're right, I'm sorry. I know you're hungry. Go eat, you two.

The Lion leaps up, gives Eve a loving lick, then he and the lioness amble over to a clump of strawberries.

Eve watches them go with curiosity… but her eyes are soon drawn to the distant **WATERFALL** on Paradise Mountain…

…and Adam at the top of it.

> **Eve:** What could he possibly be doing?

What Adam <u>is</u> doing—and has been for some time—is standing on the bank of the river pondering the thundering water and falls. Horton, at his feet, ponders with him.

Shaking his head in confusion, Adam turns away from the water just as Eve comes up the path.

Eve: *(approaching)* Something's odd. Why would a lion have too much mouth for what its mouth is actually used for?

Adam is <u>especially</u> not happy to see her.

Adam: Gee, I don't know. Why would any creature?

Eve: You claim to be the scientist.

They glower at each other… until Eve changes the subject.

Eve: What are you doing?

Adam: Discovering something that never was. That's what scientists do.

Eve: How?

Adam: Through <u>scientific</u> observation.

Eve: Of what?

Adam: The waterfall.

Eve joins him at the water's edge. Remembering Horton's advice, Adam immediately moves five steps away.

Eve: So. What <u>about</u> the waterfall?

Adam: *(irritated)* Will you move? You're blocking its view.

Eve's standing directly in front of Horton.

Eve: It's a rock.

Adam: Its name is Horton. Horton advises me on all decisions.

Eve: *(intrigued)* Really? It makes a talking sound you understand?

Adam: No. I hear Horton's thoughts.

Eve's truly impressed. She moves obediently so Horton can see.

Eve: So what, exactly, are you and Horton doing?

Adam: If I tell you, you must leave.

Eve: Why?

Adam: Because Horton thinks you need to be far away.

Eve gives Adam a noncommittal shrug, but it's enough to satisfy as Adam proudly indicates the falls.

Adam: Horton and I are about to discover how the water gets back up.

Eve: You mean after it goes over the side? Wow! Good question. I never thought of that.

Adam has—obviously—never impressed another soul. It feels good… so good, in fact, he becomes momentarily chatty.

Adam: Yeah, it seems it's always going down. But it's gotta come back up or else it'd just run out. And the coming back up part's gotta happen when we're not looking 'cause we never see it.

Eve: That's brilliant!

Adam: So Horton and me are staying here, all night if necessary, to make this new discovery—

Eve: "Horton and I."

Adam: No, not Horton and you, Horton and <u>me</u>!

Eve: No. What I meant was that "Horton and I" is the correct way to say it—

Adam: Now you <u>do</u> have to go.

Eve: But I can help—

Adam: I don't want your help.

Eve: I've got an idea…

Adam: I don't <u>want</u> your idea!

But Adam can only fume as Eve gathers twigs and tosses them into the churning whitecaps.

Eve: We put <u>things</u> in the water. They go over the falls and come back up when the water does. That way you'll have absolute proof of your observation!

Adam's anger dissipates as he thinks about this… then gets his own idea!

Adam: Only we need something bigger, so you can <u>really</u> see it.

He rushes into the forest and returns with a HUGE LOG.

Adam: Watch this.

He heaves the log into the water. It splashes and bounces happily over the falls as Eve watches it go.

Eve: Wow! That was so big.

Words that, at some level, Adam's been dying to hear. He's now the man!

Adam: That was nothing. Let's see what else…

Adam starts to look around. Suddenly, his eyes are drawn to Horton. He listens intently for a moment.

Adam: *(stunned)* Horton is a genius!

He glances at Eve. She's in awe.

Adam: Horton goes on the journey over the falls. Then he comes back when the water comes back, and tells me every detail…

Adam proudly yanks Horton from the ground.

Adam: And I won't have to stay awake all night!

Eve's awe quickly fades into a frown… a frown that Adam catches just as he's about to hurl Horton into the water.

Adam: What?

Eve: For some reason that idea feels… I don't have the word.

Adam: I know what I'm doing.

Eve: But to part with a part of you? *(to herself)* Uh oh. Another sentence with the same words in it.

Adam: *(ignoring her)* This experiment will show, once and for all, how Horton and me are not the same as you. <u>We</u> are the scientists.

Eve: *(correcting)* "Horton and I."

Adam: That's hardly the point!

With a mighty heave Adam tosses Horton into the roaring river. But instead of bouncing over the falls like the log, Horton sinks like… well, like a rock.

In the airplane, The Creator sighs as she and the silent Lucifer watch Adam's face on the TV screen fill with confusion…

Creator: You'll have to get back to the basics…

…then anger… and then, total fury!

Creator: And that would be your cue.

KAWHAM! With a press of a button Lucifer's EJECTED from the plane. As he tumbles through the sky—shrieking, wailing, flailing out of control—the countdown begins: 11 hours, 10 minutes, and 59… 58… 57… seconds.

With a wan smile, The Creator watches him go.

Creator: *(to herself)* Sorry to be rough, my friend, but it's time you understood that this one's all on you.

Back at the top of the waterfall, Adam unleashes his fury on Eve.

Adam: What did you make me do?!

Eve: Me? No! I didn't do any—

Adam: You told me to put things in the water! Where is Horton?!!

Without waiting for a response, Adam charges into the torrent hoping against hope he can save his soulmate...

Eve: Adam, no, don't...

But Adam never gets to Horton. Caught in the current, he's tossed, churned, and spun down the river... and over the falls.

Eve stares in disbelief and horror, then turns and races down the mountain. If only she can get there in time...

And thus neither one of them has any idea that Lucifer's tumbling out of the sky straight toward them.

CHAPTER 5

At the foot of the waterfall, Adam has landed in a nice peaceful plunge pool. He's okay except for being a bit wobbly and shaken. Getting to his feet he's momentarily thrilled as he looks back at the falls.

Adam: I gotta do that again!

But then he remembers Horton. His fury is fast returning when...

—Lucifer hurtles out of the sky crashing into him

—slamming them both back into the plunge pool where

—spitting and spewing, they fight like two catty teenage girls resulting in

—a sputtering face-to-face draw.

Lucifer backs off adjusting his now-sopping formalwear.

Lucifer: Apologies for the entrance. Name's Lucifer, friends call me Lou.

And—for a moment—Adam again forgets all about Horton as he carefully eyes this new creature.

Adam: What are <u>you</u>?

Lucifer: Okay, basics. I'm not a what, I'm a who.

Adam shrugs, heads to shore.

Adam: Never heard of a who.

Lucifer follows.

Lucifer: Well, a who is what I am.

Adam: That makes no sense.

Lucifer: Why?

Adam: You just said you <u>weren't</u> a what.

Lucifer tempers his fast-growing frustration.

Lucifer: Look, you have to listen to me.

Adam: Why?

Lucifer: Because I know what's best.

Adam: What's "best?"

Lucifer: For you. What's best for you.

Adam: *(shaking his head)* What's "best?"

Lucifer: Oh! You mean the word, "best." Not important. Forget it. The point is—

Adam: You have a point?

Adam examines Lucifer's clothed crotch… <u>very</u> closely.

Adam: I don't see it.

Lucifer: *(gritting teeth)* I'm here to help you with your relationship problem.

Adam is satisfied that Lucifer is pointless.

Adam: My what?

Lucifer: Look, I promise, you and the woman are, in every way, perfect for each—

Adam: "Wo-man?" What's that?

Lucifer: A woman is not a what! *(composing himself)* The woman is a "who," as well.

Adam's more confused than ever.

Lucifer: You know *(indicating boobs)* woman...

Ah! Adam nods with growing anger. "Wo-man" is the reason Horton is gone. But the assertive Lucifer is far too busy taking charge to notice Adam's simmering fury.

Lucifer: Excellent. At least you know <u>who</u> she is... You see, what I'm here to do is to make sure that you and Eve get together. You know, hang out, have fun, see where it goes...

Eve—catching her breath after her run from the top of the falls—is now watching the two men from behind a nearby bush. She's fascinated by the clothed—and apparently pointless—Lucifer, but Adam's bubbling rage is keeping her from moving one step closer.

And it's a rage Lucifer is still oblivious to as he adjusts his wet clothes, checks the location, and eyes the sun's position.

> **Lucifer:** There is, however, just the teeniest of time pressures, so you will have to do exactly as I say. No need to get into details, but we must begin immediate—

Lucifer STOPS abruptly: Adam—in his face—is about to lose it.

> **Adam:** I want nothing to do with "wo-man!"

> **Lucifer:** Okay. Understood. We'll take it slow, start with her name. Eve. You try it. Eeeeve.

> **Adam:** Eeeeve must stay far away!

> **Lucifer:** Why?

> **Adam:** Because Horton said so!

> **Lucifer:** Wait. Horton's a rock.

> **Adam:** How do you know about Horton?

> **Lucifer:** I know everything!

Eve, confused and hurt—and not yet comprehending either feeling—slowly turns away from the two men.

> **Eve:** This is not a place for me to be.

She heads to the far side of the mountain and the safety of her own forest.

Adam has zero use for his new acquaintance. Spinning away, he stomps down the path to his cave. Undeterred, Lucifer is right on his heels.

> **Lucifer:** Look. Rocks—including Horton—are "what's." They are not living creatures which are "who's"… *(to himself)* At least I think that's right. They do have molecules… *(decision)* Nope, they're inanimate. Yes. No question. Horton is <u>not</u> a "who!"—

STOP! Adam holds up his hands up in surrender.

> **Adam:** What are you saying?!

> **Lucifer:** Forget it. Is Horton is something we need to deal with?—

> **Adam:** Don't talk about Horton!

> **Lucifer:** Okay. Then how about you and Eve doing it?

> **Adam:** Eve must stay far away.

> **Lucifer:** Of course, because Horton said so!

> **Adam:** *(losing it)* <u>No</u> talk about Horton!!

Adam stomps ahead. Lucifer, dumbfounded, looks to the heavens.

> **Lucifer:** So, a rock's part of the grand plan, too?!

> **Creator's Voice:** Every<u>thing</u> and every<u>one</u> is part of the grand plan, Lou. That's why it's grand.

But Eve—more confused than ever as she arrives at her clearing—is no longer feeling like a grand anything.

> **Eve:** … everything floated, except the rock. Float or don't float, you can't have both and expect to have a natural order to things. *(growing suspicion)* And that's something a "scientist" would know! I bet he threw Horton in the water just to get rid of me. He was pretending all that other stuff.

Slowly Eve's irritation gives way to her first sorrow…

> **Eve:** What is this I'm feeling?

The feeling is "awful," but she doesn't know that word.

> **Eve:** It does not seem like it belongs in Paradise.

A tear forms… another…

> **Eve:** *(horrified)* And what is this water coming from the places I see with?

Frantic, she wipes her eyes in disbelief.

Lucifer, totally frustrated, glances again at the sun as he follows Adam through his part of the forest.

> **Lucifer:** Okay, look, for the moment, let's put the Horton business behind us… *(indicates the world)* The woman who created all this—

That stops Adam in his tracks. He's incredulous.

Adam: *(indicating boobs)* Wo-man *(indicating world)* did all this?!

Lucifer: Well, she has a female voice. Which brings me to the point.

Adam: Which you don't have.

Lucifer: Not <u>that</u> point! *(calming)* Creation requires a birth, which requires a womb, which requires a female, which in your case requires a woman called Eve!

Adam: No way... To whatever you're saying. Eve, no!

Adam spies a MOUNTAIN GOAT, takes off after it. Lucifer charges after, then slows to a halt. This isn't working... Better idea! He races off in the opposite direction.

CHAPTER 6

But, Lucifer's anxiety only increases when he finds himself with Eve for the first time. Confusion about her new feeling of sorrow has her sitting despondently by her still pond, not speaking.

> **Lucifer:** So nothing I've said even resonates?…

After his brief introduction, which he felt was quite collected and calm compared to his introduction to Adam, Eve's not responding to him at all. And with just an hour of daylight left—

> **Lucifer:** Look, you have to believe… You should really take my advice… You know, I had a great deal to do with your creation…

Whoa! Lucifer catches his reflection in the water and is horrified. His hair's a mess, and his once-immaculate white tie and tails are now dried but dirt-smudged and terribly wrinkled. No wonder she's not responding. Why would any young woman listen to someone who looked like him?

So, as he watches a pair of butterflies land on Eve's outstretched hand to cheer her up, he decides on a different approach.

Lucifer: *(proud)* You like butterflies?

Eve: Yes. They feel like… something. I don't know the word.

Whew. Got her talking at least.

Lucifer: The word is "special," and they feel special because they are. They're one of the few creatures on earth that transforms… physically… from one type to another. The rest of the creatures, of course, are not special… in that way. They remain… *(nervous cough)* the way they were when they were born… They just get bigger as they get older… The body… it develops for a reason. And that reason is… You see, it's time for you and Adam… The fact is, you're a "she," a woman, and Adam's a "he," a man, and women and men, well they…

Words fail him… so, just to keep the conversation going—

Lucifer: The butterfly was my design. It's my masterpiece, actually.

Eve: What's a masterpiece?

Lucifer: Something special you just… feel all over. Something that leaves an impression on the world.

Eve: *(listless)* I have one of those…

She sighs, holds up her cucumber.

Eve: I thought it was called a cucumber, but what do I know? *(tosses it aside)* It did make me feel all over. And, when that happened, I did make impressions in the dirt.

Lucifer: Yes… Right… So why don't we start with that very point.

Eve: I don't have a point. Adam does.

Lucifer: I know! And that's <u>exactly</u> the—*(re-composing)* My dear, do you have any idea why you're here? Why The Creator put you on this earth?…

Eve: The Creator?

Lucifer: The one who created all this.

Eve: No, how could I? The only thing I've figured out is that is that I'm supposed to be a plan that's grand. But, I don't even know what that is, so I guess I'm not much of one.

Lucifer: But you are! You're part of the grandest plan of all, The Creator's plan. And the most important part of her plan is for you to replace your cucumber… your master-piece… with Adam's… masterpiece.

Eve's confused. Lucifer indicates his crotch.

Lucifer: What he calls his "point," if you will.

Eve has no interest in that idea, but she is interested in something else.

> **Eve:** You said her. This Creator's a she... a woman?

> **Lucifer:** She is, indeed. In form and voice. Well, in form, roughly half the time.

> **Eve:** So she and I are the same?

> **Lucifer:** There are certain differences, but essentially, yes.

> **Eve:** Well, if we're the same, she already experienced Adam's point on the second day, and she was... I don't know the word.

But the mere thought prompts a <u>BIG YAWN.</u>

Lucifer's stunned, then pissed. He fires a glance heavenward...

> **Lucifer:** Bored? Really? Name one other specie you've created that gets bored with sex!...

In the Spruce Goose, The Creator shakes her head.

> **Creator:** *(to herself)* That one's not mine, Lou. That one's all yours.

Evening's on its way as Adam, back in the vegetable patch, gathers cantaloupes for the night's entertainment. He thumps and squeezes them for ripeness, choosing only the very best.

Lucifer—furious with Adam—rushes up, out of breath.

Lucifer: I've been looking all over creation! Where have you been?!

Dirt now smudges Lucifer's face, his hair's askew, and thorns and brambles have made small rips in his clothing. He despairs as he watches the sun sinking toward the horizon.

Lucifer: Don't <u>ever</u> leave your cave without telling me!

Adam: What?! Why?

Lucifer: Because I have no idea where you are, we have no time, it'll be night soon—

Adam: Duh! I figured out night after the first day… and night. What makes you think you're so smart?

Lucifer: Because I know things.

Adam: You know how water comes back up?

Lucifer: Back up?

Adam: The falls.

Lucifer: Ah. It doesn't. There's this thing about evaporation and clouds and moisture, took eons to design—

Adam: *(incredulous)* The water <u>doesn't</u> come back up? Ha! You're useless.

Adam's had enough. He takes off, four cantaloupes in hand.

Lucifer: Wait, I only know <u>very</u> <u>important</u> things…

He races after Adam, catches up.

Lucifer: One of which is that the human race does not come into existence unless you and Eve do it. And do it soon.

Adam: "Human race?" "Existence?"

Lucifer: Yes. Other… stalwart… men like you need to be here. *(under his breath)* Some women as well.

Adam scowls, which Lucifer takes as his disapproval of women.

Lucifer: And that's okay because someday humankind will realize how amazing and wonderful women are…

But that's not the reason for the scowl. Adam stops.

Adam: Other <u>men</u> will be here?

Adam's eyes narrow as looks possessively back at the cantaloupe patch.

Adam: Other men not wanted. And no more talk about woman. Woman stays <u>far</u> <u>away</u>!

He walks on. Lucifer follows, gets a sudden idea, but approaches it gently.

Lucifer: Adam? Why do you think Horton said that women should stay far away?

Adam: Don't know.

Lucifer: Yes you do. Why, Adam?…

Adam: Well… because.

Lucifer: Because why?

Adam: Because when she's far away, I can't hear her.

Lucifer: And why don't you want to hear her?

Adam: Because I lose focus. From what I want. Which she <u>doesn't</u> want because <u>she</u> doesn't have wants, <u>she</u> has needs—

Lucifer: How do you know?

Adam: She told me this morning. And she doesn't even know what they are!

Lucifer's eyes light up.

Lucifer: Well then, sounds like we'll just have to give those needs some definition!

Thus, as the sun sets, a frantic Lucifer is back pleading with Eve in the clearing by her pond. Leaves cling to his hair and there are now big rips and holes in his coat and pants.

Lucifer: … so, even if you <u>believe</u> you don't need him for that… isn't there something?

Eve: I can't think what.

Eve's despondency is gone for she has a new project! On her hands and knees she's carving individual words in pieces of wood with <u>her</u> writing rock. Words like: tree, grass, lion, water, cow…

A smiley face adorns "cucumber." They're friends again.

Lucifer, now curious, comes closer.

> **Lucifer:** What are you doing?

> **Eve:** I'm making a dictionary.

> **Lucifer:** Oh? Oh! Very smart.

Eve is pleased at the compliment.

> **Eve:** I will be labeling everything in Paradise. Perhaps Adam might read the dictionary someday and learn things, whereupon he might be able to talk with some intelligence. At that point he might become <u>useful</u>, but certainly not needed.

> **Lucifer:** "Intelligence?"

> **Eve:** It's a new word. Having the faculty to reason and understand knowledge which, of course, he woefully lacks.

Lucifer notices another pile of wood with carved words. "Better" and "worse" are visible, but on top of this pile is the word "lonely."

> **Lucifer:** What's this group here?

> **Eve:** Those I know the words, but not the meaning.

Lucifer picks up "lonely."

> **Lucifer:** Maybe Adam could help you with some of them. This one in particular.

Eve scoffs at that idea, continues to work.

Eve: He's hardly a word-gatherer… *(changing the subject)* So, why are <u>you</u> here?

Lucifer: I'm here because, somehow…

His words trail off as he tosses "lonely" back on the pile. For the first time defeat looms in the distance.

Lucifer: I have to save human existence…

He pulls an **APPLE SEED** from an inside pocket of his now not-so-immaculate tailcoat, looks at it slowly as he turns it over in his fingers.

Lucifer: Without you two eating the apple.

Eve: What's an apple?

Lucifer: A fruit. It's red, grows on a tree, looks enticing.

Eve: What happens if you eat it?

Lucifer indicates the "lonely" pile.

Lucifer: You'll know the meaning of all those words. And then some.

Eve: *(perks up)* Really?

Lucifer: Eventually you'd know the meaning of every word ever invented.

Eve: Then I should find this apple and eat it if I'm writing a dictionary.

Lucifer: Well you can't, because the apple's not gonna happen.

Eve: Why not?

For a second there's a softness in Lucifer's eyes as he looks at Eve… but then it's back to all business. Mind racing—and totally distracted—he puts the seed back in his pocket…

> **Lucifer:** Because, as the angel in charge of human happiness, I have decreed there will never be an apple in Paradise…

…not realizing the pocket now has a hole in it. Unnoticed by either, the seed drops to the ground.

> **Eve:** Well, if there's not gonna be any apple, then what's the point in talking about it?

> **Lucifer:** Indeed.

Eve refocuses on her work. Lucifer, dejected, silently disappears into the woods. He's getting nowhere. Time for him to refocus on Adam.

> **Eve:** *(finishing her sign)* Okay. That's it.

Eve looks up. No Lucifer. She shrugs, arranges her words in neatly organized piles, and sets her writing rock aside.

> **Eve:** We'll do more tomorrow.

Eve stands. Night is falling and the **FULL MOON** is appearing above the horizon. Eve gives it a warm and welcome smile.

> **Eve:** Time to go to Moonview Plateau.

In her two weeks of life, Eve has watched the moon grow from a tiny sliver to a magnificent, miraculous, brilliant beauty of the night, and she truly adores it. So, grabbing the "Moonview" sign, she heads up the pathway.

Just as she disappears into the woods, a glorious **BIRD OF PARADISE** gracefully swoops to the ground, snatches the apple seed in its beak, soars back into the sky, and follows behind Eve at a discrete distance, unnoticed.

CHAPTER 7

Hours later, on a perch high above **MOONVIEW PLATEAU**, the Bird—still unnoticed, still holding the seed—watches over Eve as she gazes longingly at her beloved moon.

At the same time, the moonlight streams into the man-cave where the disheveled Lucifer—fuming at Adam—is desperate!

> **Lucifer:** … let's do it again. There's not that much to remember! You've been here only two weeks!!

> **Adam:** And you've been here all night asking me the same questions!

Adam, exhausted and pissed, sits slumped in front of his centerfolds.

> **Lucifer:** *(to Adam)* Well, guess what? We're gonna find the answer if it <u>takes</u> all night. What is the one thing in this world that Eve needs?!

> **Adam:** Who cares?

Lucifer: You do, I do, The Creator does. Fulfill a need, get closer, create desire, and the two of you—

Adam: I told you, I have no idea. If it's not her cucumber—

Lucifer: *(frustrated SHOUT)* It's not! The cucumber just happens to be… handy!!

Adam instantly slaps his hands over his ears.

Lucifer: Why can't you listen?!

Adam: Noises should be far away!

In the Spruce Goose, The Creator watches the two on the TV.

Creator: *(to herself)* He's right Lou. Same questions over and over…

She glances at the clock, shakes her head. Four hours and two minutes left.

Creator: *(to herself)* Time to up the ante a bit.

Back on earth, as Lucifer—momentarily silent—shakes his head in dismay, Adam—with some caution—drops his hands.

And in the Spruce Goose, The Creator chuckles as she watches a new idea hatch in Lucifer's brain.

Lucifer: *(to Adam)* You said noises. Noises! The noise of her voice—

Adam: And yours should be <u>far away</u>!!

Lucifer: Yeah, I get that. But Adam, that time you were up the tree—

Adam: How'd you know about that?

Lucifer: I know everything. What "noise" did she say to you <u>that</u> day?

Adam: If you know everything, then you'd know what she said.

Lucifer: I didn't say I <u>remembered</u> it all! At the precise time of that event I was a bit preoccupied with a thing called an airplane—

Adam: Well, guess what? I don't remember, either!

Looking for distraction Adam grabs a cantaloupe, rolls it around in his hands with expectant longing.

Lucifer: *(beginning to boil)* Adam, those words were enough to keep you up that tree. You have to know what they are!

Adam: Well, I don't.

THWOP! Lucifer kicks the cantaloupe out of Adam's hand smashing it into pieces against the wall.

Lucifer: Tell. Me. Now!

Adam eyes the shattered cantaloupe in horror.

Adam: Why'd you do that?

Lucifer: I will crush every cantaloupe in Paradise unless you start talking.

Lucifer grabs another cantaloupe and is about to send that one flying—

> **Lucifer:** For the last time, what were the words that drove you up the—

> **Adam:** *(desperate)* Okay, stop! "Pretty" was the first, "Ro… romantic" was the second, "L… L… L… Love" was the third.

> **Lucifer:** *(sudden panic)* She said the L word??!!!

> **Adam:** I don't know what they mean. I just knew I needed to be up the tree.

> **Lucifer:** *(not listening, terrified)* That's impossible. I was positive I eradicated emotions when I… Sure, "pretty," "romantic," those are adjectives, they're gonna appear at some time, but "love?" Nononono…

He catches himself, stops his rant , turns back to Adam.

> **Lucifer:** Son, do not concern yourself with "love." "Love" is <u>not</u> coming to the Garden of Eden. Ever.

> **Adam:** Fine by me.

And now Lucifer is all peaches and cream.

> **Lucifer:** However, knowing these words as I do, it sounds like she <u>is</u> interested in you.

> **Adam:** *(scoff)* Not hardly.

> **Lucifer:** What do you mean by that?

> **Adam:** The words weren't about me.

Lucifer: What?

Adam: I told you. She doesn't care about me other than to have someone to talk at. Those words were about the moon.

Lucifer: The moon?!

Adam: Every night she goes up on the mountain and watches the moon until she falls asleep.

Lucifer: How do you know?

Adam: I… uh… I watch her sometimes. She's still far away, though.

Lucifer: That's it! Stay right there.

Lucifer charges out of the cave. Safely out of earshot he looks up.

Lucifer: You there?

Creator's Voice: Of course. I'm always "there," Lou.

Lucifer: Good. I want an eclipse. Now!

Up in the Spruce Goose, The Creator just shakes her head.

Creator: You want what?

Lucifer: The moon is all I've got to bargain with—

Creator: So you want a <u>lunar</u> eclipse? Are you sure you know what you're asking for?

Lucifer: Of course I know. I was at eclipse class… most of it anyway.

Creator: Actions can have unintended consequences.

Lucifer: I'm aware of that! I still need the moon to disappear!

Creator: *(rolls her eyes)* Alright. But only because experience can be such a grand teacher.

Lucifer: Enough with the riddles, already!

Creator: Okey dokey. Get ready.

With a quick turn, Lucifer swipes at the moon as if he were in charge. And, as if on his command, the moon begins its passage into the earth's shadow.

Lucifer: Excellent!

In the Spruce Goose, The Creator is long-suffering.

Creator: *(to herself)* No, Lou, it's not. Not even close.

At the same time, up on Moonview Plateau, Eve's aghast. Her beloved moon is disappearing before her very eyes.

Eve: No! No!! Nonononono…

Charging back and forth she jumps, waves, screams, and pleads, but the moon just continues its inexorable shrinking.

The Bird of Paradise still watches over Eve, the apple seed still in its beak.

Desperate for any solution, Eve turns and races down the mountain path.

Eve: Hellppp! Adaammm! Helllppppp!

And, just as she disappears, the bird swoops to earth, buries the seed in the soft earth with its beak, and flies off.

Back in his man-cave, the despairing Adam is on his knees trying to reassemble the cantaloupe pieces when Lucifer charges back in.

Lucifer: Okay. Get ready.

Adam: Huh? For what?—

Lucifer: For Eve. She's coming. Hurry. Get up, get up!

Adam leaps to his feet… and instantly backs away. He wants nothing to do with whatever scheme Lucifer's come up with now.

Lucifer: No, no, you don't understand. This time she's gonna <u>need</u> you. This time she <u>neeeeeds</u> your help. This time, <u>you</u> can do something <u>she</u> can't.

Adam: Like what?

Lucifer: Like, return the moon.

Adam: Huh?

Lucifer: You'll see. Trust me. The moon has disappeared and you're going to make it re-appear.

Adam: "Disappear?" "Reappear?"

Lucifer: For which Eve will be very grateful.

Adam: But how do I?—

Lucifer: You... uh... *(whatever)* make circles with your hand.

He shows Adam who starts to imitate, but Lucifer stops him.

Lucifer: Not yet, wait 'til you're with her.

Eve: *(from outside)* Adam... Adam!...

Eve is racing down the mountain path. Her voice is still far away, but it's close enough to make Adam back further into the cave. Lucifer counters by shoving him toward the entrance.

Lucifer: Okay. New words. You like new words?

Adam: No.

Outside, Eve is sure her world is crashing. Gasping, panting, she's now only a minute away. She runs, stumbles, lurches forward.

Eve: Adam!!!

Inside the cave, Adam panics.

Lucifer: Stay with me, guy. The words I'm about to tell you are going to save mankind. The words are "uh" and "huh." Say them!

Adam: Uh. Huh.

Lucifer: Faster.

Adam: Uh-huh.

Lucifer: Again.

Adam: Uh-huh. Uh-huh.

Lucifer: Very good. No matter what Eve says, say those two words. They'll work like a charm.

Eve, breathless and frantic, bursts into the cave.

Eve: Adam… Adam… Look! LOOK! It's the moon… I need you—*(catching herself)* I need a scientific… *(plea)* The moon is disappearing… Can you just come see?

Adam says nothing… until Lucifer prods him.

Adam: *(not moving)* Uh-huh.

Eve: Can you come see <u>now</u>!

Two more prods.

Adam: Uh-huh, uh-huh…

But he's still not moving. Exasperated, Lucifer prods <u>and</u> shoves Adam toward Eve.

Adam: Uh-huh, uh-huh, uh-huh…

And before Adam knows what's happening, Eve has grabbed his wrist and dragged him outside.

Eve: It happened when I was at Moonview Plateau. We've gotta go up there.

Adam: Uh-huh.

There's no time to lose. As Eve pushes/drags Adam to the mountain path, Lucifer—inside the cave, energy spent—collapses against the wall.

Lucifer: I am <u>not</u> cut out to be a matchmaker.

In the Spruce Goose, The Creator instantly RE-WINDS the images on the screen.

Lucifer: (*on TV, repeating*) I am <u>not</u> cut out to be a matchmaker.

Creator: (*to herself*) Well, I'll be…

She rewinds, plays it again.

Lucifer: (*on TV, repeating*) I am <u>not</u> cut out to be a matchmaker.

Creator: (*to herself, pleased*) Okay, that's a start.

CHAPTER 8

Distressed and panicked, Eve virtually drags Adam the last ten yards as they reach the open expanse of Moonview Plateau.

> **Eve:** *(pointing to sky)* See?! It's almost gone!

Adam, huffing, puffing—and at a complete loss—looks up. The sky is awash with stars, but only the faintest shadow of the moon.

> **Eve:** Can you do anything?
>
> **Adam:** Uh… huh.
>
> **Eve:** Can you do it now?
>
> **Adam:** Uh… huh.
>
> **Eve:** Then do it! Please!!
>
> **Adam:** Oh… yeah… right.

Still trying to catch his breath, he makes weak circles with his hand.

While Adam is doing his level best to bring the moon back, Lucifer—outside the cave—waits for nature to take care of the very same thing. But something's wrong. The moon's not coming back.

Perturbed, Lucifer flips at the earth's shadow with his hand as if demanding it disappear. To his surprise the shadow does not respond. He flips more forcefully. Nothing. Flip/flip—still no moon.

Furious, Lucifer FLIPS everywhere. FLIP/FLIP/FLIP/FLIP/FLIP. Forwards, backwards, flips within flips… Nothing works.

Lucifer: What's happening?! *(heavenward)* Where are you?

Creator's Voice: You talking to me?

Lucifer: Of course I'm talking to you!

Creator's Voice: I beg your pardon!

Lucifer: Sorry. Meant no disrespect. But what are you doing?!

In the plane, The Creator's innocent.

Creator: Nothing.

Lucifer: What did you do with the moon?

Creator: I didn't do anything you didn't ask for.

Lucifer: It's not coming back.

Creator: I know.

Lucifer: Do you know why?

Creator: Of course.

Lucifer: Then tell me!! Eclipses only last minutes!

Creator: <u>Solar</u> eclipses last minutes. <u>Lunar</u> eclipses take hours. In this particular situation the moon will be in complete darkness for one hour and forty-seven minutes.

Lucifer: *(sputtering)* Well… okay… We'll still be alright… They'll… they'll just have to wait it out. I'll bluff 'em through it. This is a foolproof plan—

Creator: Want to guess how much time you have left?

Lucifer: Well, uh, with the moon gone…?

The Creator glances at the clock.

Creator: Three hours and sixteen minutes.

Lucifer: That still leaves one hour and twenty-nine minutes after the moon comes back. He'll still be a hero, and there'll still be enough time for them to—

Creator: Really? This moon sets before the sun comes up. And the sun comes up in <u>forty-one</u> minutes.

REALITY! Lucifer gasps.

Lucifer: So, the "pretty, romantic" moon—

Creator: Will not be seen until tomorrow night. When it will be…

Lucifer: Too late. *(losing it)* No! Nononono. That's not fair. That's not fair at all. You didn't warn me! I can't think of everything!!

Creator: Yeah, I know. *(to herself)* That's kind of the point of this exercise.

On Moonview Plateau the moon has now been completely covered by the earth's shadow. But from Eve's perspective it's just gone. So—totally bonkers—<u>she's</u> now waving Adam's arm around!

Eve: He said a circle right?… You sure it was a circle?… Was it a circle this way… Or that way?… This way or—

Adam: What are you doing?!

Adam yanks his arm back.

Eve: I'm doing exactly what you said <u>he</u> said to do!

Adam: Yeah? Well, what if <u>he's</u> not a scientist?!

Eve: Huh?

Adam: What if he doesn't make sense? Which, I found, is most of the time. What if <u>he</u> stole the moon?

Eve: No. You think?

Adam: Well, <u>I</u> didn't steal it. And, for sure, you didn't. Who else is there?

Eve: But why?

Adam: Well… uh… that's the part I don't know.

Eve: *(not listening)* Unless…

Eve's eyes are widening in stunned amazement. She looks past Adam…

Eve: Unless he wanted to leave something just as beautiful in its place.

Over Adam's shoulder, a mere fifty feet away, the most extraordinary bush is growing right before Eve's eyes. No, it's not a bush, it's a tree! Shimmering, shining in glorious radiant light—the only tree on the plateau—it's stretching to its full height when—

POP! One beautiful apple appears on a single, glimmering limb.

Eve: *(stunned)* It's… It's…

Indescribable.

Eve: Instead of the moon, he left an apple. He must want me to know all the words now. But why?

Adam: What are you talking about?

Adam spins to look. Whoa! The size and beauty of the tree stagger him.

Adam: What in the…? How did you know about this? This is… scientific. This is stuff I'm supposed to know!

But Eve isn't listening. She's left Adam behind and is headed directly for this new fascination.

Of course, back outside Adam's cave, Lucifer—with no idea what's actually happening on Moonview Plateau—is still bitterly complaining to his boss.

Lucifer: No, no, no, no! I had it all set up.

Creator: And it didn't work. So, you ready for Plan B?

Lucifer: What?! You knew?

Creator: C'mon, Lou. You <u>still</u> using that line?

Lucifer: It's just one small seed—

Creator: That will create the one glorious apple of Love.

Lucifer: And all the bad stuff that comes with it...

Lucifer pats the outside of his tailcoat with confidence. He thinks the seed's still safe.

Lucifer: Which is why it is never going to be used! Those two don't deserve those awful feelings. I've still got time. I'll figure something out—

Creator: Why'd you bring the seed, Lou? Really?

Lucifer: Like you said, Plan B.

Creator: So, even you weren't sure of your plan.

Lucifer: No. I mean yes. Of course I'm sure. We're making excellent progress. Just a little setback here and there. As a matter of fact, I am so sure of my success that I will now decree that the seed will no longer be Plan B. As a matter of fact, it's not even gonna be the "last resort." It's gonna be no resort at all because…

With a flourish, he reaches inside his tailcoat…

Lucifer: I'm going to swallow it!

Huh? The seed's not there!

Lucifer: What?!… How in the world?!…

Panicked, he searches all his pockets—no apple seed.

Lucifer: What did you do now?

Creator: Me? Nothing.

ZIP! A shiver of anxious fear again races down Lucifer's spine.

Lucifer: Stop saying that! You stole the seed.

Creator: Now, that would not be very Creator-like.

Lucifer: You and I were the only ones who—

Creator: Lucifer! The seed was not stolen. It was given.

Lucifer: Do not talk in riddles!

Creator: Don't you have better things to do?

Lucifer: As a matter of fact, I do. I'm simply going to find the children and—

Lucifer glances up at Moonview Plateau... and FREAKS! The brilliant light FLOODING the mountain could mean only one thing. **THE APPLE TREE!**

> **Lucifer:** Wha...? Omigod, my babies! *(yell)* No, stop you two! Eve, Adam, stop!

Frantic, he charges for the mountain path.

The apple tree is even more surreal in the splendor of the rising sun. With limbs out of reach and a sheer, shimmering, glass-like trunk, it's impossible to climb.

Eve and Adam, transfixed, stare up at the radiant Apple.

> **Eve:** Everything I need to know is in that one piece of fruit.

> **Adam:** But you said <u>he</u> said not to eat it.

> **Eve:** It's meant for me. It's here in place of my moon.

> **Adam:** Which I <u>didn't</u> bring back like he told me I would. Why am I even part of this thing?

> **Eve:** Like you said. Most of the time he doesn't make sense.

Eve jumps—several times—trying to grab the apple, but can't. Adam enjoys her... jumping... until she stops.

Eve: I can't get it. You try.

Adam: Why? It's not for me.

Eve: I need you to.

"Need"—the magic word.

Adam jumps—which Eve enjoys watching—but he can't reach it either.

Adam: It's no use.

Eve's perplexed, but <u>not</u> giving up.

Eve: I've got an idea.

Eve positions Adam directly beneath the apple and clambers up on his back like a ladder... which Adam can't stand...

Adam: Stop! Stop it!

He pulls her off.

Eve: Please Adam. I really, really need your help...

Again, the magic word.

Eve: I can't do this without you.

Adam softens and thinks.

Adam: Alright. But must do this scientifically. *(idea!)* What if we tried this?

Facing Eve, he lifts her in a way so that his face is nestled in a place that—to some—might be called awkward.

It's also awkward for Eve and Adam… but not entirely unpleasant.

Adam: How's… that?

Eve: Little higher…

There's a strange intriguing hoarseness in their voices, but neither recognizes it for sexiness.

Adam: Higher… uh… okay…

Adam spots the Apple, shifts Eve upward. But, for him, the Apple is now secondary. What's primary is his growing appreciation—and his growing appendage—caused by this new close-up view of her.

Eve: *(husky)* Little more… almost got it.

Adam, happily, shifts her even higher…

Adam: *(to himself)* It's nice to be needed.

But, just as his face is about to be buried in a place it's never been before, Eve SCREAMS at something she sees in the distance!

Adam: Wha… What?

Eve: The lion! Something's happened… Put me down, quick!

Scrambling her way out of his arms, Eve accidentally kicks Adam right in his groin. He doubles over in pain.

Adam: Ow, oh ow! Ow,ow,ow,ow!…

But Eve, racing across the plateau, doesn't hear Adam's agony.

Adam: Owowowow! I don't know this word, "ow." Ow, ow, ow, ow, ow, ow.

The Male Lion bursts out of the woods urging Eve to follow.

Eve: C'mon Adam. The lion needs us.

Eve charges into the forest after the lion, leaving Adam alone in his misery.

As he watches her go, Adam does manage to straighten up a bit… just not quite upright. Convinced he'll never be the same, he glares at the offending apple as this new and terrifying feeling called pain overwhelms him. Hobbling to the path leading <u>down</u> the mountain he reminds himself firmly—

Adam: Wo-man must stay far away!

Lucifer, of course, is huffing and puffing his way <u>up</u> the same path, so it's only natural that somewhere in the middle the two meet…

Lucifer: *(horrified)* My boy, what happened?—

Adam: No <u>wo-man</u>, no way!

Bent almost double, Adam hobbles down the path past Lucifer as fast as his bowed legs can take him. He can't get to the safety of his cave soon enough.

Lucifer: *(after him)* The apple… Did you two?—

Adam: *(over his shoulder)* No way <u>ever</u>!!

That, of course, gives Lucifer a ray of hope. The Apple may still be intact! He lets Adam go and charges up the path to Moonview Plateau...

Moments later—and out of breath—he staggers to the Tree, looks up. The Apple's still intact, glowing on its branch.

Lucifer almost cries with relief... but what's happened to Eve? Desperate, he turns in circles. Finally he spies the path taken by Eve and the lion.

> **Lucifer:** If there's still time, there's still hope.

Cheered by the thought, he races in the direction taken by Eve.

But, up in the Spruce Goose, The Creator can only sigh as she watches her misguided underling charge ahead.

> **Creator:** *(to herself)* Without the apple? More like hopeless, Lou.

CHAPTER 9

Minutes later the panting, exhausted Lucifer stumbles into the lion's den where Eve now sits with three brand new, adorable LION CUBS in her lap. Papa and Mamma Lion look on approvingly.

Lucifer: What's this? What are you doing?

Eve: This is called a "home." I believe all creatures are supposed to have one…

Eve giggles as she gently holds and pets the sweet babies.

Eve: It's where the bigger ones stay until they find the little ones growing in the forest. Or maybe they find them under rocks, I'm not sure. Anyway, after they're found, they all stay in the home together.

A Cheshire cat grin spreads across Lucifer's face.

Lucifer: Yes, yes, yes. Homes are delightful. And delightfully… domestic. Perhaps you and Adam—

Eve: Wait!…

Eve has a sudden brainstorm as she cuddles a fuzzy cub.

Eve: I don't need Adam. I can use you!

Lucifer: *(aghast)* What?! No, that would never do—

Eve: But you're big enough—

Lucifer: Size isn't everything. I want to make that perfectly clear—

Eve: And you're right here! Right now!

Lucifer: That has nothing to do with it. Adam is—

Eve: I <u>don't</u> <u>need</u> Adam. <u>You</u> can help me get the apple.

Lucifer: *(relieved)* Ah, the apple is what you're... *(but NO! backing away)* Nonononono. No apple my dear, I already told you and, yes, you do need Adam. You need Adam very much. Now, you just continue playing "home" with those adorable little creatures and thinking lovely "homey" thoughts, and I'll be back in no time.

Before Eve can say another word, Lucifer's GONE! She shakes her head in dismay, then looks down at the little ones.

Eve: *(to the cubs)* That Lucifer creature isn't much good for anything, is he?

The curious cubs WHIMPER back at her.

But there's a different kind of whimpering going on back in the man-cave, and this time it's coming from Lucifer.

Lucifer: *(to Adam)* … please, you gotta go back. She's primed and ready. Nothing happens if you two aren't together!

Adam points defiantly to his crotch. His pain is still fresh.

Adam: And <u>that</u> doesn't happen if she stays far away!

Lucifer: She didn't mean to kick you. You'll be fine—

Adam: Who says? You? You said the moon would come back.

Lucifer: That was a simple misunderstanding.

Adam: You don't know anything!

That does it. Now Lucifer's pissed.

Lucifer: You know what? I don't think humans are worth it. You're one twelve-millionth of all living things on earth. You're tiny, miniscule, meaningless, not even that. Why don't we just <u>not</u> have you? Why don't we just stop everything right now? Why don't we just pretend you never happened? You won't be missed. You're nothin'.

Again Adam's totally lost, but this time it's Lucifer's tone that gets to him.

> **Adam:** I... I don't know who you are... or why you're here. But what you just said makes me say "ow" inside...

He brushes at a tear—another strange thing for him.

> **Adam:** And makes water come out of the holes I see with!?

Adam breaks down, sobbing. Lucifer's made him feel awful, and crying is new... and scary.

> **Adam:** What have you done to me?

Lucifer chokes back his own tears. Forcing efficiency, he approaches Adam, puts a semi-comforting hand on his shoulder... but from a distance.

> **Lucifer:** I... Look, I shouldn't have said that... You would be missed. You would be missed very greatly. All I ever wanted was for your lives to be perfect.

"Perfect." Another word Adam doesn't understand. But Lucifer's tone is softer so Adam wipes away his tears.

Lucifer, regaining <u>his</u> composure, casually checks the bright sunlight streaming into the cave. Yikes! Just two hours and twenty-six minutes left! Immediately he's back to all business.

> **Lucifer:** Okay. This can still happen. You said, when you were holding her up to get the apple, you thought she changed, was a bit—

Adam: Different, yeah. I guess. I don't know.

Lucifer: And you were…?

Adam: Oh, I was different…

He nods to his crotch in despair.

Adam: But it hasn't happened since!

Lucifer: And it won't if you don't try!

But, as The Creator notes—watching the TV in the airplane—Adam's still plenty reluctant.

Adam: *(on TV, to Lucifer)* I… I don't think so.

Lucifer: *(on TV, to Adam)* Look, I made this perfect world for you! Can't you make it perfect for me?

Creator: *(to herself)* Really Lou? You made this world?

Adam: *(on TV, to Lucifer)* I don't know what to do.

Lucifer: *(on TV, to Adam)* Just try harder this time!

As Adam sighs "okay," The Creator grabs a small recording device…

Creator: *(to herself)* That's it…

Speaks into it.

Creator: Note to self. Send angel to earth named Einstein. Have him describe insanity as doing the same thing over and over again and expecting different results!

And, as Lucifer and Adam leave the cave and head for the lion's den, The Creator shakes her head. There are simply no more words.

Unfortunately for Lucifer and Adam, Eve isn't in the lion's den. She's returned to her clearing, busy with her word signs. So now the two of them—panting from their exhaustive search—watch her from behind a nearby tree.

Lucifer: I was seriously not made to gallivant all over The Creator's creation.

Adam: Huh?

Lucifer: Never mind…

Recovering from his exertions, Lucifer nods to Adam's crotch.

Lucifer: How's the…?

Adam: Okay.

Lucifer: See, I told you. Maybe now, you'll listen?

They look out at Eve. Today she's <u>not</u> writing. Today she's trying—without success—to "drill" a hole in the sign using a small stick as a drill bit.

This particular sign is "Grassy Bush." Eve stops, sighs with resignation. She's making no progress.

Lucifer, with a quick glance at the sun, whispers intently to Adam.

> **Lucifer:** This is it! You're on. Go!

> **Adam:** But, what do I do?

> **Lucifer:** Don't ask. Don't think. Just <u>do</u> what comes naturally!

He shoves Adam into the clearing. Adam balks but—at Lucifer's insistence—he turns to Eve—

> **Adam:** Uh… hi.

Eve looks up.

> **Eve:** Oh… hi.

For reasons neither understands, Eve and Adam are now far more attracted to one another… although Adam is still somewhat cautious.

> **Adam:** So… what's going on?

> **Eve:** Oh, nothing… 'Cept, I'm trying to make a hole in the sign. The animals keep dragging them away when I leave the signs on the ground…

Adam's presence is affecting Eve. Her words don't come as easily.

> **Eve:** You know. When the signs are moved, "tree" ends up next to a bush and "bush" ends up…

She trails off as she gazes up at Adam, clearly standing taller than the last time she saw him.

Adam: Next to… a tree.

Eve is affecting him as well.

Eve: Exactly…

But, in a nanosecond, Eve's back to the matter at hand.

Eve: Anyway, I want to make a hole in the sign so I can hang it on a branch, or something high enough. That way it can't be moved, so in no time at all…

As she continues to talk, Adam starts to back away… but is stopped by Lucifer's whispered hiss.

Lucifer: Stand. Your. Ground!

Eve takes a breath, thinks for a moment.

Eve: But I'm not having much luck. You think you could try? It might be one of your scientific things.

She extends the stick to Adam.

Lucifer: *(whisper)* Yes. YES! Take it. Take it!

Adam glares at the hidden Lucifer, approaches Eve, takes the stick. Turning it over in his hands he looks at it from every angle… Then a brainstorm!

Adam: Ah ha! Let's try this.

He kneels on the ground in front of the sign.

Adam: Come here.

He indicates Eve to kneel in front of him, hands her the stick. Awkwardly they figure out it works better if she kneels between his legs, so they're snug... An act Lucifer cheers in whispers.

Lucifer: Yes, yes!...

Eve: *(husky)* So... uh.... Now what?

Adam: Hold the stick between your palms.

Eve complies.

Adam: And now we do this.

Placing his hands over hers, Adam bends them over and guides her hands to the sign.

Eve: *(shallow breath)* Very... scientific...

Adam: *(shallow breath)* Now... just follow me.

Slowly he begins to move Eve's hands back and forth causing the stick to spin in her hand, much like the motion the scouts use for starting fires.

To Lucifer, however, this act is downright phallic.

Lucifer: Oh yes... Yes, yes...

Adam: Faster now...

Hands move faster...

Adam: Faster...

Lucifer's in ecstasy...

Lucifer: Yes, yes, yes...

But things are moving much too fast for Eve. She spins out from under Adam and leaps up, still holding the stick. But it's not that she didn't like what was happening. She nods to Adam's crotch.

Eve: So, I... uh... I see your point... and I want you to know that I find it...

Oh my, quite extraordinary...

Eve: But I...

Adam stands as well. Now only semi-erect, he's more than a bit confused. Eve stares for a second...

...but then, waving the stick, she's again all business.

Eve: But I really must do the signs. They're quite necessary for our lives...

Adam, however, isn't listening. Instead, he's pointing excitedly <u>at</u> the sign.

Adam: LOOK!

Eve looks, and yes, there is a tiny indentation.

Adam: It worked!

Eve: Wow! So, what I need to do is to start slow... let the hole form around the stick... Then go faster... and faster...

Adam: And faster... Yeah, something like that.

But neither one knows where to go from here.

Adam: So...?

Eve: So. Okay. I... I got this.

Adam: Okay. Well then, I guess I'll—

He indicates the woods where Lucifer remains hidden.

Lucifer: *(to himself)* Nonononononono...

Eve: *(to Adam)* I'll... I'll see you.

Adam: Yeah, sure. I guess. Maybe.

Adam turns to leave.

Eve: That was a pretty smart thing you came up with.

Adam: *(shrugs)* No big deal.

He stomps into the woods. As he does, Lucifer grabs him.

Lucifer: Are you insane?!

Adam: What? I give her nothing, she doesn't need me. I give her everything I know, she doesn't need me <u>anymore</u>. She doesn't have any needs I can do anything about.

He grumbles off.

Adam: This is over. I quit. I'm done.

Lucifer: *(after him)* No, Adam, you can't quit...

Lucifer's at a loss. He watches Adam go... then—fitfully glancing at the sun—he charges out of the woods to Eve.

CHAPTER 10

Eve glares at Lucifer rushing toward her... but continues with her drill-stick.

Lucifer: Eve, listen, you've gotta believe me, the moon <u>will</u> come back—

Eve: Which you wouldn't know unless you took it.

Lucifer: Look, I promise—

Eve: Whatever that means.

Lucifer: What can I tell you?—

Eve: You can tell me when you'll put the moon back.

Lucifer: Tonight. The moon will be back tonight.

Eve stops her drilling.

Eve: And if it's not?

Lucifer: It <u>will</u> be—

Eve: *(drilling again)* Well, I just might not be here.

Lucifer: It won't matter. You'll be able to see it from wherever you are. Wait. What did you say?

Eve: *(ignoring Lucifer's last statement)* Ha! That's what you know. You can't see the moon behind trees and big mountains. And sometimes there's a big poofy thing in the sky and you can't see it then either.

Lucifer: *(desperate)* Look, you can't leave.

Eve: You know, I don't think you know much at all. You took away a perfectly good moon and, in its place, left an apple that nobody can reach—

Lucifer: There's a logical explanation—

Eve: You know what else? I don't think I'll listen or talk to you anymore... Wow. I haven't said that to any creature.

Lucifer: Eve, no, don't! We've gotta talk. You're my last hope—

Eve zips her lips, goes back to drilling her sign... faster... faster... faster.

Slumped in defeat, Lucifer trudges back into the woods and disappears. Time's running out and he needs to be alone, think of something new.

But something very new is happening as Eve continues to drill. First it's just a wisp of smoke, then another—more of a cloud this time—and it's not long before the sign-hole begins to smolder…

Which Eve doesn't realize until a small **FLAME** leaps up!—

Terrified, she drops her drilling stick and scrambles for the safety of a small boulder… Cautiously, she peers out—

The flame has disappeared. Curious, yet apprehensive, she approaches the sign again, eyes it carefully…

Slowly she picks up her drilling stick, examines <u>it</u>, then proceeds to drill again… faster… and faster—

Another flame! Eve jumps back, but not as scared this time. She waits for a moment, approaches again, drills again…

Another flame, another jump!… But now Eve's more thrilled than afraid.

Seeing a small reddish glow in the hole, she cautiously touches it with her finger…

> **Eve:** Ow! Owowowowowowowowowowow!

Hopping around the clearing trying to stem the pain, she instinctively plunges her hand into the nearby pond. Great **RELIEF!**

> **Eve:** What was that? And what was that word "ow?"

She has no answer but, as the pain eases, the thrill of discovery returns. She looks at her finger as she pulls it out of the water, then looks back at the sign. Astonishment and great pride spread across her face.

> **Eve:** I've discovered something… something that never was! I… I'm… I've got to tell Adam!!

Leaping to her feet she races off, screeches to a halt, tears back, props the smoldering sign under the <u>actual</u> grassy bush, and dashes into the forest…

Thus, it's only moments before the sign <u>and</u> the grassy bush are in flames. As the bush is surrounded by rocks, the fire would seem to be safely contained. And it is—

Except for **TWO SPARKLING ASHES** carried by the winds in opposite directions.

The FIRST SPARKLING ASH is carried to Moon-view Plateau where it settles in a clump of grass a hundred yards from where Lucifer sits, alone and forlorn, at the mountain's edge.

The broken-down angel is almost in tears. What to do? What's left? What can work? He glances over at the Apple in the tree thirty yards away.

> **Lucifer:** You are <u>not</u> happening…

But—with his focus on the Apple—Lucifer fails to see that a slow-growing, semi-circular grass fire is about to entrap him <u>with</u> the tree.

The SECOND SPARKLING ASH now hovers at tree height above Adam, who sits listlessly in front of his cave sighing to himself.

> **Adam:** So, I'm not needed… who cares?

Eve, excited and breathless, rushes up.

Eve: Adam, you won't believe… *(no response)* Don't you even care what I have to say?…

There's no acknowledgement from Adam but, at the same time, the ash—unnoticed—floats to a feathery tree just down the hill from the two of them.

Eve: *(miffed)* Look. I made a discovery. I created something that never was.

Adam: So?

Eve: That means I'm a scientist, too.

Adam: Be what you wanna be, it doesn't matter.

Eve: But you were the one who helped me. You showed me how. We could discover everything. Together.

Adam: Why do you have to know everything?

Eve: Because it's important.

Adam: What happens when there's nothing left to know?

Eve: Well, that's going to be at least a few more days.

Adam: What're you gonna do then?

Eve: I, uh… Well, I don't know.

Adam: See, now that's the kind of thing Horton would have known, because Horton <u>did</u> know everything. And you made me throw him in the river because you don't want anyone to know more than you do.

Eve: That's not true. And I did not <u>make</u> you do a single thing!

Even Eve is surprised by the strength of her response. But it unleashes a long held-back torrent—

Eve: Okay, let's say Horton did know every-thing! So, if he did, he knew when you threw him into the water he would sink!

Them's fighting words. Adam leaps to his feet.

Adam: What did you say?!

Eve: I had nothing to do with it! It was Hor-ton's idea, remember?! Horton knew he had to be out of your life.

Adam: Why?! Why would he do that?

Eve: Because he knew he was in the way. He knew that we… you and I… were supposed to… Horton knew that the two of us are <u>both</u> supposed to be a plan that's grand!

Suddenly, the wind SHIFTS…

Adam: That makes <u>no sense</u>!

…and a shower of sparks blown from the feathery tree—now ablaze—rains down on Adam.

Adam: What the… Ow! Ow! Ow!

Eve: *(to herself)* That's the same word <u>I</u> said…

Eve turns to the tree. OMG! Her little red ember has somehow become a huge blaze. Trying not to freak out, she points at the fire.

> **Eve:** Um... I... well... That's my discovery. Sort of.

> **Adam:** *(furious)* You did this? You're making me say this word "ow?" <u>Again</u>?!

But Eve sees what Adam doesn't; the fire is spreading.

> **Eve:** I... I...

And spreading fast.

> **Adam:** Go away! I never want to see you again.

Eve, stunned, doesn't move. Dancing flames are reflected in her eyes.

> **Adam:** This is <u>my</u> cave. Go!

Eve's panic leaves her speechless, but Adam still doesn't have a clue.

> **Adam:** Really?! Forget it, then. You can have the cave. <u>I'm</u> gone.

Adam spins, charges off, but is stopped by a SUDDEN wall of flames. Another direction, no good... Another direction, no...

They're both trapped. Together! Surrounded by fire and singeing sparks, there's nowhere to go...

Except WATERFALL POOL. Eve sees the path, grabs Adam by the arm.

Eve: C'mon.

Adam: *(pulling away)* No! Get away!

Eve: Fine! I will. You stay as long as you like!!

She's off. But, another shower of stinging sparks is all Adam needs. With fire licking at his heels, he immediately follows after.

Adam: Ow! Ow, ow! Ow!

Eve looks back, sees him.

Eve: I know what to do. C'mon…

They charge forward. A turn… they've made it! Just ahead, the waterfall spills into its peaceful plunge pool.

Eve races for the water, jumps in. Adam hesitates momentarily but, with the flames closing in, jumps in after her. The water's up to their necks.

And only then does Adam understand as relief comes to his scorches.

Adam: Ahhh!… How'd you know about this?

Eve: It happened to me.

She holds up her finger.

Adam: You said "ow" too?

Eve: Yeah. I did.

Adam: I… I didn't know.

Momentary awkwardness… that's soon forgotten as they take in the surging fire around them.

Adam: What… what can we do?

As their eyes slowly follow the ever-widening circle of flames they both turn… and soon have their backs to each other.

Eve: I have no idea.

Confused and frightened, each takes a step back without realizing that it's bringing them closer together.

Adam: Maybe we just stay here…

Eve, stunned speechless by the blaze, just nods… takes another step back.

Adam: Become fish…

A final step… and a shocked GASP from each as their backs touch! Both stand perfectly still, afraid to move.

Eve: Right. Fish… that can't breathe.

At Moonview Plateau however, Lucifer stands scowling in defiance at the fiery blaze that now traps him.

Lucifer: This is absurd!…

He charges madly into the flames. Scorched and singed, he quickly retreats to relative safety. And now he's furious.

Lucifer: *(to the fire)* No! Nonononono!! You don't get it. I'm an angel! Fire has no power over me.

Creator's Voice: But pain does, it seems.

The Creator is nowhere to be seen, but the **VOICE OF THE CREATOR** comes from somewhere in the flames.

Lucifer: Huh? You're here?

Creator's Voice: *(bored)* I'm everywhere, Lou. Haven't you heard?

Lucifer: What's going on. Why is this happening?

Creator's Voice: I'm multitasking.

A flame leaps out, singes Lucifer on the butt.

Lucifer: OW!!

Creator's Voice: It appears you need a reminder that you're not quite as immune to pain as you might have thought. And, of course, pain can come in all <u>sorts</u> of ways.

Lucifer: I know that!

Creator's Voice: Really?

Another flame leaps, this time scorching Lucifer's hand.

Lucifer: Yikes! Cut it out.

Creator's Voice: Maybe you should get someplace safe?

Lucifer: And I suppose you have some suggestions.

Creator's Voice: Dealing or not dealing with pain is simply a choice, Lou.

Lucifer: Yeah? Look around. There's no place the fire isn't!

Except under the apple tree. With everything else engulfed in flames the circle of lush green grass surrounding the tree is <u>not</u> burning.

Lucifer: No! No! NO!! I know what you're doing and I refuse!—

Creator's Voice: Suit yourself.

Zap/singe/scorch!

Lucifer: Owowowowowow!

Caution to the wind—and yelping all the way—Lucifer dashes through the flames to the safety of the tree.

Whew. Relative calm. But, with the fire raging around him and the clock running down, he looks up at the Apple and grimaces.

Lucifer: Okay. Now what? *(no answer)* We're wasting time here.

Creator's Voice: Really, Lou? Seems like you've been the one wasting time.

Lucifer: I beg your pardon! I have done everything in my power—

Creator's Voice: Whose power?

Lucifer: Okay. Point taken. But this fire thing is beyond the pale.

Creator's Voice: Not really. Every angel-in-training has a weak spot. Keeps them humble. Keeps them from thinking they're perfect. Keeps them from thinking they're me. Humans were modeled after that, but then you missed that class too.

Lucifer: That class was in the four-thousandth, three-hundredth, and twenty-third year of training!

Creator's Voice: Nobody said being an angel was easy.

Lucifer: Why are we even having this conversation?!

As if to answer that question, The Creator chuckles... then calmly strolls out of the flames, obviously unscathed.

Lucifer: *(stunned)* You're really here?

Creator: "They" are gonna say I was, anyway. Might as well make it official.

Lucifer: But I thought—

Creator: It's time, Lou.

She indicates the Apple hanging on the tree.

Lucifer: No... I can... I can still do this. I will, I promise. But, I gotta get going—

Creator: No. You don't. What you've got to do is what should have been done hours ago, days ago, weeks ago.

Lucifer: I just... No... Please?... *(he breaks)* I... I'm sorry. I didn't mean to tinker, it was just... I couldn't see them suffer. I <u>love</u> them.

Creator: Yet you've done everything possible to push them away from one another and from you.

Lucifer: I wanted them to have the perfect world.

Creator: But I <u>created</u> them to be loved for their <u>imperfect</u> parts and deeply admired for their differences. And the reason I did was so they could see in the other what they lacked in themselves. For each will need the other to fulfill the grand plan...

Lucifer perks up. Best not miss the "grand plan" this time.

Creator: They are to have domain over this, my incredible creation. By their <u>choices</u> they will decide if the earth—and everything on it—flourishes or withers, lives or dies. That is the only reason they are here. Can you please see that, because this particular grand plan cannot happen—those choices <u>cannot</u> be made—until both of them understand <u>what</u>?...

Lucifer: *(contrite)* L... l... love... *(last plea)* Look, there must be something—

Creator: There is nothing else. Do what you must.

Lucifer—in one final, desperate effort—tries to think of something, <u>anything</u>… But it's useless.

Lucifer: *(miserable)* Alright. I guess.

He sighs, looks up, and reaches for the apple. As he does, the branch bends toward him bringing the brilliant fruit within reach.

Lucifer picks the apple, missing The Creator's compassionate smile. But as the branch rises to its original height, Lucifer does note that a peaceful rain has begun to fall.

Creator: Lou, what I'm asking for is an act of faith.

Lucifer: I know. *(sigh)* You know what you're doing.

Creator: Yes. But the faith I'm asking you to have is faith in our creations. Faith that Eve and Adam will always know that the very survival of the human race will depend on the togetherness that love brings. And faith that this knowledge will be <u>their</u> greatest gift to humankind. But, to do that, they themselves must know a love that is divine.

Lucifer: Divine?

The Creator: Pure. Spiritual. Without ego. A love found only in their hearts. And they must marry that exquisite, open, and <u>unselfish</u> love to the beautiful bounty of the <u>selfishness</u> they carry in their bodies—their true desires, their wants, their needs, and their passions. For it is this primordial marriage of divine love and pure passion that will be the source of life. This eternal oneness will be the origin of all human creation.

Lucifer nods, pretending to understand, but what he's most interested in is that the rain is putting the fire out, so at least all that pain stuff will be gone.

And what did she say about different <u>sorts</u> of pain? Did he miss that class too? He shakes his head. It's all too confusing. The only thing he is absolutely sure of now is that there is no way he is ever getting his angel wings. He has never felt more useless.

CHAPTER 11

As the fire dies in the downpour and the rain stops, Eve and Adam climb out of Waterfall Pool, look around in wonder and amazement.

Eve: *(big relief)* Glad that's over.

But Adam's amazement quickly shifts to anger.

Adam: This was you. You did this! Your creation, your <u>discovery</u>, made me say ow again!

Eve: That wasn't what I wanted—

Adam: You didn't <u>want</u> to do any of this. It still happened—

Eve: But—

Adam: Guess what? <u>I've</u> got a new discovery. I've discovered I don't like saying "ow." And since <u>you</u> seem to be the reason I'm saying it all the time, <u>I'm</u> going to go far away, once and for all.

Eve: Where… where will you go?

Adam: Maybe I'll go to the edge of this place where the stars are close to the ground and stay with them. Or maybe I'll go in another direction where there's <u>another</u> Paradise of cantaloupes and where sheep and goats stand still! Wherever it is, it'll be a place where a man will never have to say "ow" again!

He stomps off. Eve, more befuddled than upset, suddenly remembers, calls after him—

Eve: Perhaps? Before you go? Can we try and get the apple again? I think it would help—

Adam: Yeah. Help you learn more words. That makes no sense.

But, as Eve watches Adam disappear into the charred forest, her tears come again…

Eve: *(to herself)* Especially when there will be no one to tell the words to…

This time she doesn't even bother to wipe them away.

Eve: *(to herself)* It's this <u>life</u> that makes no sense.

Lucifer sighs, then nods to The Creator as he weighs the Apple in his hand.

Lucifer: I'd best go find them, I suppose.

Creator: Are you sure, Lou? Are you sure you understand this time?

Lucifer: No. But you're the boss and, as you said… faith. Blind faith in my case, but—

Creator: Thank you.

Lucifer: Where are they?

Creator: Back where it all started, at the top of the waterfall. Eve's looking for her moon.

Lucifer: *(forlorn sigh)* In the daytime.

Creator: She has a great deal of hope.

Lucifer: And Adam?

Creator: He's in his same hiding place, watching her. He has a great deal of hope as well.

Lucifer glances at the sun.

Creator: Forty-five minutes left.

Lucifer nods and sets off sloshing through the debris. The Creator watches him go.

Creator: *(to herself)* You're almost there, Lou. Just a little further.

Eve at the top of the waterfall—eyes red from crying—continues to search the morning sky for her missing moon.

Adam, hidden in the bushes, looks on… until he hears something. He turns as the demoralized Lucifer joins him, shaving off a piece of the apple with a small pen-knife.

Lucifer: Heard you were going on a journey.

Adam does his best to ignore him, but curiosity gets the upper hand.

Adam: How'd you know?

Lucifer: I know every… I know some… I may not know much, but I do know that.

Lucifer's a mess. Burned, scorched, his right pant leg is now in shreds. Twigs and briars have long since claimed his hair.

Lucifer: And—since you are leaving—you'd better eat this.

His heart breaking, Lucifer offers Adam the piece of the apple. Adam, instantly suspicious, shakes his head.

Lucifer: It's so you won't get hungry on the trip.

Ah! Well, that's different. Adam takes the apple piece, gobbles it down.

Lucifer: From now on, pay no attention to anything except what you feel *(touches Adam's heart)* in here.

Adam's feeling something already.

Adam: Like with my fish?

Lucifer: Like with your fish… Count to one-hundred, then come out.

But, as Lucifer starts to leave, Adam grabs him.

Adam: I can only count to two.

Fragments—tiny fragments—of the grand plan are starting to jell for Lucifer. It's only the very beginning, but this time he gives Adam a gentle smile.

Lucifer: Of course. Two. Eve and you. Okay, just wait 'til Eve eats <u>her</u> piece, then come out.

Lucifer joins Eve in the clearing. However, as he hands her a piece of the apple, his approach is entirely different.

Lucifer: Look, I know what I said, but I… I reconsidered.

Eve eyes the apple piece with excitement, but she still doesn't trust Lucifer.

Eve: You mean I really will know <u>all</u> the words?

Lucifer: Sadly, yes.

Eve: I'll know that word too?

Lucifer: *(nods)* But you'll know "happiness" first. Great, great happiness. And that's as it should be.

Eve: Well, alright. But we're still not talking.

Eve eats the apple piece, slowly at first, then with increasing enthusiasm as she feels herself changing somehow. And, with her last swallow, her eyes turn to…

Adam, who takes two steps out of the bushes and stops. This is an Adam we haven't seen before. This Adam is a man, a man in rebirth, struggling in his cocoon, afraid to be born, yet afraid not to be.

Before him stands someone he's never known before. And that someone is the woman Eve. Proud, erect, and powerful, she's the most glorious Eve he has ever seen. In an instant, fiery passion races through his body. His needy desire wants to take her with every ounce of his being.

But something—a mysterious feeling he has never had before—is holding him back. If he could describe it, he would call it empathy, a simple exquisite tenderness, a sweet selflessness. All he wants to do now is to <u>listen</u> to her, to protect and help her, to honor her in any way possible.

All he wants to do now is to give this woman everything she wants.

"But I can't take and give at the same time," Adam frets, afraid to move. "Which do I choose? And what if I choose the wrong one?"

Eve, is stunned by the sight of this new Adam. "He's beautiful," she thinks, "more beautiful than I've ever seen him. But he's leaving for another place, and I have better things to do. I have words to learn." She turns, starts off.

Lucifer sighs, looks up.

>**Lucifer:** *(to the Creator)* They're all yours.

He heads in the opposite direction, disappearing from view.

But a sudden—and also new and mysterious—feeling makes Eve stop. Slowly, she turns around, now looks at Adam with curiosity.

> **Eve:** Why are you still here?

> **Adam:** *(fearful nod)* I don't know what to do.

> **Eve:** About?

> **Adam:** You. And me.

Eve's new feeling is strange. Like she can understand what he's saying without him actually saying the words.

> **Eve:** I feel the same way.

Adam nods.

> **Eve:** Then let's do nothing, except what we
> are doing right now.

What they are doing—for the very first time—is looking directly into each other's eyes. The feeling is both vulnerable and intrusive, but also enticing. This give and take, back and forth—even from across the clearing—leads them to a place they have never been, the outskirts of one another's souls.

And—without a word being uttered—here they find common ground in the shared passions between them: an unfettered desire for knowledge, a deep need for the truth, a constant yearning for companionship…

Which confuses them both even more.

> **Adam:** <u>Are</u> we the same?

Eve: It would seem so. At least in some ways. What does it mean?

Adam: It means we can be… friends. I just thought of that word. I'm not sure what it means.

Eve thinks for a minute, then her eyes sparkle.

Eve: Friend: a person you like and enjoy being with.

Adam: *(tentative)* Okay. I think I can be a friend.

This new awakening alleviates the lingering tension. The two look around, marvel at their surroundings, as if seeing them for the first time.

Eve: Isn't it magnificent?

Adam: Isn't it beautiful?

But, as their eyes return to each other, something else happens. There's now the possibility of sharing these surroundings with someone they seem to like very much…

Adam: <u>You</u> are magnificent.

Eve: And <u>you</u> are beautiful. Inside and out.

…and one whom they now have an urgent desire to know even better.

Adam: *(softly)* What's happening?

Eve: Feelings. Feelings of connection

Adam: What is this called? Do you have a word?

Eve: Love.

Eyes glistening with happiness, Eve takes a step toward Adam.

Eve: True love.

Adam: *(a revelation)* True love: when the wants and needs of the other are more important than your own…

Adam finally gets it. It's not all about him anymore. He takes an answering step toward Eve.

Adam: *(further revelation)* … where there is no difference between giving and taking.

Eve agrees with his truth.

Eve: True love feeds passion…

Her words draw them together like a gentle magnet…

Eve: The two become one, inseparable.

…a trusting, ecstatic heat begins to build…

Eve: When passion and true love are inseparable, that is when love is called divine.

…building to an unbearable intensity engulfing them both.

Adam: And divine love is the place where pleasure has no end. It is the place of you and I… together.

Less than a foot now separates them. Eve looks deeply into Adam's eyes, and smiles. What she sees is openness, trust, honesty…

Eve: I love you.

…but also an almost childish embarrassment?

Adam: I love you…

Tears brim in Adam's eyes. As he gives her a longing smile, he indicates his body with dismay.

Adam: But I don't know how to show it.

Eve ponders this, then she too has her own revelation. Taking his hand in hers…

Eve: It begins like this…

She reaches up and tentatively kisses Adam… Both back away quickly, giggling in soft amazement, but Adam nods with new understanding.

Adam: A good beginning.

Another kiss, and another. And another—this time slower… and deeper—as love and passion, together, entwine the two of them.

In the bushes—out of sight—Lucifer sits slumped against a boulder. He eyes the half-eaten apple. Heck, nothing better to do, so <u>he</u> takes a bite…

Suddenly he's hallucinating. Or is he? In his mind's eye he sees lights—an incredible dance of lights. He can't look away.

From somewhere in the heavens comes the—

> **Creator's Voice:** Amazing, isn't it, Lou?

> **Lucifer:** What is this? What's going on?

> **Creator's Voice:** The Mother and Father of all humankind are finding divine love.

Lucifer's mind is blown. He's never known anything like this. What he's looking at is—

Silhouettes of Eve and Adam exploding into pulsating flames of passion as their kiss uncovers the energy of love buried deep within their souls.

Suddenly the kiss stops. The two pull away, gasp at each other in wonder. In disbelief they tentatively reach out, touch the other's lips. Warm desire SURGES again. Moving from lips, they begin a soft exploration of the other's body and find lightness, aching magnificence, and unfathomed sensuality. Golden laughter and gasps of desire accent sensations both unbearable and exquisite in places where they can't—where they won't—ever stop touching.

Slowly Eve lowers the two of them into the soft grass. She guides Adam's hand back to those places, directs his motion and touch.

Adam follows her lead. "How can anything—anyone—be so wonderful," he marvels. He searches for a word to describe... and finds it! Bliss.

Adam's tenderness fuels Eve's passionate heart. She feels the rightness of this. Of them.

Adam does too. Slowly, he moves Eve's hand to his special place. His want soars! Gasping, he slows his breathing and calms… until his want matches her need… until, together, their wants and needs become a single flame of desire and love soaring higher… and higher… and higher…

Until want and need become must. Now they <u>must</u> get closer. Now they <u>must</u> become one. The urgency grows. They can't get close enough. They gasp, they surge, they heave, they give and take, take and give…

Convulsion, EXPLOSION!!! Massive arcs of bursting color blanket the universe illuminating the All and Nothing—The Alpha and The Omega—that embeds forever in the souls of Eve and Adam the essence and experience of ecstasy and life…

Eve and Adam are one…

CHAPTER 12

Lucifer's in tears. He's never seen anything as beautiful as the love Eve and Adam have shared with one another. He looks to the heavens for guidance…

> **Lucifer:** You were right. Their love is truly divine. I didn't know.

At which point The Creator chooses to appear directly in front of him.

> **Creator:** *(kindly)* You didn't know what, Lou?

> **Lucifer:** In… in their oneness, they see you.

> **Creator:** In as much as I am divine love, that is true.

> **Lucifer:** And will all who are here in the future see you as well?

> **Creator:** All will have that ability… The love of Eve and Adam is to be one of total acceptance, of total belonging, of total completeness. Eve and Adam <u>are</u> Divine Love. Thus, every future child on earth will know that he

or she began with that divine incarnation, with that perfect love. And it is <u>this</u> knowledge that is to be the foundation of human civilization.

Lucifer: *(drying his eyes)* I've been a fool.

Creator: Understanding love will always be a challenge.

Lucifer: Why?

Creator: So that it will be eternally searched for, and never forgotten. It's that important.

Lucifer nods and sighs.

Lucifer: I was like Adam in a way. We both thought everything centered on us.

His admission hurts. Tears brim again.

Lucifer: I thought I knew best. I thought I could fix everything so they would never be hurt.

Creator: As <u>you</u> are now.

Lucifer: *(wiping eyes)* I don't understand.

Creator: The hurt of you being forgotten. Of you never again existing in their world, of their world becoming completely indifferent to an angel called Lucifer—

Lucifer: *(unconvincing)* No, no I'm... I'm good. I get it. No worries. We can just move on.

Creator: *(ignoring him)* And that is simply not going to happen.

Lucifer: Our objective was those two, and they're fine. Wait. What did you just say?

Creator: <u>You</u> gave them the apple. You will <u>never</u> be forgotten.

Lucifer nods… slowly acknowledging… and silently accepting credit where no credit is really due.

Creator: And yes, those two are fine. Almost. You see, it's one thing for the <u>two</u> to be in love. It's another for them to love those <u>other</u> than themselves. That they still need to learn. And rather rapidly.

Lucifer: You mean she's—

Creator: Twins, actually. So, you can see the urgency.

Lucifer frowns. A funny feeling tells him this is not going to end well.

Creator: As such—since all is good—you wouldn't mind just ambling over and letting them love <u>you</u> for a few minutes, would you? Before we go?

Lucifer's mind races. No way this is a good idea.

Lucifer: I don't think… It's not really… There's no reason… When the little ones come along they'll be so cute—

Creator: Since there's not another "other" in Paradise at the moment, Eve and Adam can only learn how to love others from their creator.

Lucifer panics. It was only a few hours ago the two exiled him from their lives. Sure, he gave them the apple, but that wasn't really his idea. No, they don't want anything more to do with him, period. And who can blame them?

> **Lucifer:** Wait! You said, "learn... from their Creator." That's you—

> **Creator:** Which will take humankind a few hundred thousand years to figure out. But, right now, you and your apple are it. <u>You</u> are the one who gave birth to who they are today.

Lucifer gulps. There's no way out. His every fear returns. What can I do? It's clear I don't have enough love. I failed the two of them...

What if I fail them again? Then I fail all humanity...

And then I will have failed my Creator. Completely. And there can be nothing in the universe more horrible than that.

Lucifer's fears aren't helped when he finds Eve and Adam in the clearing. Sitting in the grass—eyes only for each other—there's no interest in him whatsoever.

Lucifer "ahem's" for the third time—finally gets their attention—and makes a feeble attempt at cheerful...

Lucifer: Hi guys.

...bombing miserably. He winces as the two peer up at him through dazed eyes. "They don't even recognize me," he frets. But then Adam gives him a lazy snort.

Adam: "Guys?" That's what <u>you</u> know. Eve's a woman...

And an indignant woman at that. She glares at Lucifer, turns to Adam.

Eve: You're right. He <u>doesn't</u> know anything.

Adam: And I am a man. That's a shortened version of woman.

Lucifer: You're right, you're both right... *(to himself)* You probably know way more than I do now.

Satisfied, Eve and Adam go back to cuddling <u>and</u> ignoring him.

Lucifer: So I just want you to know that I'm leaving...

No response...

Lucifer: This is... uh... good-bye...

...no response...

Lucifer: You won't see me anymore...

...no response.

Lucifer shakes his head. Another defeat—he's totally worthless. The tears come quickly this time so, turning away, he heads for the anonymity of the forest.

Lucifer: And… I'm sorry for everything.

That gets Eve's and Adam's attention! They look to each other in confusion. In a flash they're on their feet.

Adam: Wait!

Eve: The word, "sorry." What does it mean?

Lucifer stops, turns back…

Lucifer: It's a feeling I never wanted you to know.

Eve and Adam are stunned. It's the first time they actually see the TEARS streaming down Lucifer's face.

Adam: *(gulps)* This feeling makes water come out of the holes that you see with.

Eve: *(agreeing)* <u>That</u> feeling we already know…

Eve and Adam tear up in empathy.

Adam: We don't want any creature in paradise to feel that way.

Eve: We don't need to know your words… *(brushing at her tears)* to know that you need us.

Slowly—hand in hand—Eve and Adam approach Lucifer, gently wrap their arms around him. In his misery, he simply lets them. There's nothing more to do. Their heads each rest on his shoulders.

Eve senses it at first. An almost a hyper-aware feeling.

Eve: *(to Lucifer)* We will help you.

Lucifer sobs, saying nothing, but Adam senses the feeling too.

Adam: *(to Lucifer)* We will protect you.

A sudden new understanding flows from Eve to Adam and back again. They clasp their arms tighter around Lucifer.

Adam: *(to Lucifer)* We will love you.

Eve: *(to Lucifer)* Forever. And ever.

Lucifer melts. There are no defenses left. The walls are down. The love from his two charges fills him up, fills him to overflowing…

And in a final moment, Lucifer surrenders. His arms sweep around Eve and Adam embracing the two in a tight, tight hug. There are no more words, only feelings of give and take, take and give. Feelings of a deep and passionate love between the three of them.

Amid grateful sobs, Lucifer looks heavenward for <u>his</u> Creator.

Lucifer: You planned all this, didn't you?

Creator's Voice: *(chuckles)* Multitasking, but yes. You're part of the grand plan too, my friend.

Lucifer: *(stunned)* You're… you're giving me a second chance?

> **Creator's Voice:** Always. There's going to be a lot more for you to do.

Lucifer breaks.

> **Lucifer:** I… I love you.

> **Creator's Voice:** That's nice to hear. It's been a while…

Was that a catch in the Creator's voice?

> **Creator's Voice:** Understand, I will always love you.

> **Lucifer:** I do… I can… now.

> **Creator's Voice:** Good. So, get back to your kids. There's a few minutes left.

Back in the embrace, Lucifer starts LAUGHING! Laughing for joy. He never felt so good, so right, so loved. And he never had so much love to give.

Indeed, dear reader, it was at that exact moment that all the love for everyone and everything that would ever exist on planet earth came into being. All from that one circle of love that was Lucifer Eve and Adam.

And there are tears everywhere. Even in the Spruce Goose The Creator dabs at her eyes as the digital clock makes its one final click—**11:11**.

But, the strange thing is the tears are different now. These are tears of happiness, and Adam is the first to notice. He slows, then stops the festivities in amazed wonder and curiosity.

Adam: *(to Eve)* Water that comes from the holes you see with could be sad—

Eve: *(agreeing)* Sad: causing or associated with grief or unhappiness…

Adam: Or happy—

Eve: Feeling pleasure and enjoyment because of your life or situation.

Adam: So, what's the deal with that?

Eve: *(intrigued)* I dunno. *(to Lucifer)* Do you know?

Lucifer shakes his head.

Lucifer: Still workin' on that one, myself.

Eve: *(to Adam)* This we need to talk about.

Adam: Okay.

Lucifer: And it's time for me to go, anyway.

Adam: You alright now?

Lucifer: I am. And thanks.

Eve: For what?

Lucifer: For being you.

Eve thinks about that for a moment and smiles, happy inside.

Eve: I like that.

Adam: *(whisper to Eve)* What does he mean?

Eve: *(taking his arm)* I'll explain, but first we need to work on this "sad/happy" thing.

Eve and Adam each give Lucifer a little wave. He gives a little wave back, then watches as—snuggling together—the two head down the mountain. As their voices trail off, there's a noticeable lump in Lucifer's throat. He <u>is</u> sad. It <u>does</u> hurt. But, now? That's very much okay.

Lucifer: *(to himself)* Good luck, kids. I'll miss you. *(after them)* You may want to cover up a bit. Temperature's gonna change.

CHAPTER 13

Back in the Spruce Goose, The Creator pilots the aircraft through the starlit heavens. She turns to the disheveled Lucifer now back in the co-pilot's seat. He's deep in thought.

Creator: Glad you finally figured it out.

Lucifer: I had no idea.

The Creator: Most of those who end up on earth won't have any idea why they are there, either.

Lucifer: *(affirming)* To be love.

The Creator: *(shakes her head)* To become love. It takes time.

Lucifer: And those two will be okay?

The Creator: *(nods)* Pretty much. Want to take a look?

Lucifer: *(thrilled)* What?! Can I? Can I really? But… but only those sure to get angel wings have ever been given a glimpse of the future!

Creator: I'm confident. It may take a few more years—

Lucifer: YES!

Lucifer's ecstatic. In a FLASH he's out of his seatbelt, parading around the cockpit like Jubilation T. Cornpone!

Creator: Put your seatbelt back on!

"Jubilation" quickly scurries back to his seat, embarrassed.

Lucifer: *(subdued)* Yes ma'am, of course. Sorry. Back to Eve and Adam. How many years should I?…

He reaches for the dial on the TV.

Creator: I dunno. Try nine hundred.

Lucifer's impressed, twirls the dial.

Creator: There's going to be a weird book— with absolutely no sense of time—that will "say" they lived that long, anyway.

Lucifer stops the dial at **900 hundred years from now**. He flicks a switch. Instantly the screen fills with the image of a small, ancient, but active, village. Adults go about their final daily tasks as children play in the late afternoon sun.

Quickly the image morphs to the inside of a **SHEPHERD'S HUT**. Simple, but warm and inviting, there's a small fire, a pot, a water jug… and a straw bed where Eve—<u>extremely</u> old—is nearing the end of her journey.

Adam, also bent and withered, holds her hand.

Eve: Did we do it, Adam? Did we live a life of love?

Adam: We tried. Did our best.

Eve: *(agreeing)* Our very best.

Adam: Our very best has been <u>our</u> love.

There's still a twinkle in Adam's eye.

Eve: *(chuckles)* Some things <u>do</u> last a lifetime, don't they? Our eight-hundred-ninety-fifth birthday? Remember?—

Adam: *(agreeing)* When they all barged in, even the great-great-great-great grandkids... *(smiles)* I remember all our birthdays, <u>and</u> the days in between.

Eve: Am I still better than a cantaloupe?

Adam: Way better. And how 'bout cucumbers?

Eve's eyes brighten with fascination.

Eve: With you it was always different. Never the same...

Adam: But it always led to that same beautiful place. It was awesome.

Suddenly Eve's eyes widen...

Eve: *(stunned)* Oh my!...

She's seen the light... and a new revelation.

Eve: It <u>always</u> will be awesome...

Radiantly beautiful in this last moment...

Eve: Adam, it always <u>will</u> <u>be</u>! We're just beginning!

And nodding with confirmation and great joy, Eve allows her soul to leave her body.

Evening approaches as Adam, kneeling in a quiet, peaceful clearing on a hillside, smooths the earth around Eve's new resting place. It's the one last time to be near, the one last time to touch…

He pauses a moment, reflecting… then nods to himself, okay.

Struggling to his feet, Adam looks out at the snow-capped mountains in the distance and the lush valley below. Pairs of animals trundle across the plain, drink at the banks of the lazy river, and graze as the sun sets on the horizon.

Adam: The world is a better place because you were in it, my dearest. That's all that ever mattered.

He smiles at the first glimpse of the full moon, and a tear forms in his eye…

Adam: Your moon's come back.

…but his gaze then returns to his beloved.

Adam: My perfect love, my perfect lover. Wherever <u>she</u> was… <u>that</u> was Paradise.

And a host of beautiful memories floods Adam's ancient face as we come to—

- 149 -

ALMOST THE END

EPILOGUE

Time has flown. It's now only about two thousand years ago. It's taken a good bit of effort but today—in front of The Creator and the entire body of heavenly hosts—Lucifer is finally getting his angel wings. There's an excited mumbling throughout the crowd.

> **Crowd:** "Did you hear, Lucifer got Earth!" "Wow, only the very best get assigned earth." "That's 'cause it's the toughest." "The lucky—" " "No lucky, he's good, he earned every bit of it…"

Lucifer's grin stretches from ear to ear. Dressed in his dapper best, he starts to raises his right hand, then quickly corrects to his left to take his final pledge.

> **Lucifer:** *(to The Creator)* For all eternity, at your request, I Lucifer, will return to the density and matter of earth for whatever period of time you desire. The only and sole purpose for my return will be to help others. This is my true joy and my greatest exaltation. I seek naught but to always be of service to you.

As the crowd ERUPTS, The Creator smiles as she pins a tiny replica of the Spruce Goose on Lucifer's lapel. But as she gets closer to his ear, she whispers—

Creator: We need to talk.

It's later. As a joyous heavenly party rages around them, The Creator and Lucifer are huddled in a corner.

Creator: … I'm just putting you on alert. Jesus is there now so hopefully things will work out. But you may have to handle this yourself. There's this guy on earth—actually a bunch of them now—who can't believe that Lucifer Eve and Adam is, and always will be, the source of eternal love and happiness—

Lucifer: Why? What happened?

Creator: That's a whole other story. The point is these guys have written books that define crazy things called religions, and those religions have split the humans into tribes and factions and hatreds and jealousies instead of keeping them together. In these books, they've first turned you into a snake, and then put you in charge of a place they invented called hell, which ironically, is full of flames—

Lucifer: What?!

Creator: Some have actually shifted the blame to Eve for what they now call misery! It's a mess. But the most ridiculous thing of all? In a long and absurd litany, they've made sex some sort of sin and made <u>me</u>, The Creator, a permanent <u>he</u>! With a long nasty beard and lightning bolts of deadly vengeance!

Lucifer: Wow. Sounds like I'll just have to go back and let them know what the truth actually is.

The Creator: Thanks. Spoken like a true angel. Keep an eye on it for me, won't you?

Lucifer: Absolutely. But, before I do, can I just spend a little more time at the party? It's been a long time coming.

The Creator thinks for a moment, then nods.

The Creator: No problem. Just don't wait until things get <u>totally</u> out of hand.

THE END

Praise for Peter Wilkes's book,
A Woman Called God

"A wise and lovely book that should be widely read"
—**Jean Kilbourne, creator of the *Killing Us Softly* film series and author of *Can't Buy My Love* and *So Sexy So Soon***

"Charming, unthreatening and delivers a wham-o message. Subversive to the status quo, the big R (Religion) and the big P (Patriarchy), with its simple, easy to grasp premise."
—**Jean Shinoda Bolen, M.D., psychiatrist, internationally known author and speaker**

"Bravo to this tour de force to Mr. Wilkes and for daring to bring a hopeful funny perspective on a delicate subject matter leading too many times to conflict and war. *A Woman Called God* is calling for: Peace Now!"
—**Emmanuel Itier, film director, *FEMME: Women healing the World***

"Thank you for sharing your wonderful book with me. I can't tell you how aligned it is with my beliefs and what I teach. I have studied this ideology for years and am a huge proponent of the message. I wholeheartedly support what you are doing and the way in which you are doing it."
—**Sheila Kelley, author of *The S Factor***

"Sometimes simple is better. *A Woman Called God* is a case in point. In it, Wilkes plays with the oversimplified male construct of God that we sometimes find in the Bible and flips the story to imagine what that kind of construct would look like as female. The result is a God that looks a lot like the God many of us know. For those who struggle with the feminine in God, this may be just the tiny book needed to help you make the last step. For those who already are there, this may be the exact tool you need to help a friend."
—Rev. Mark Sandlin, co-founder of *The Christian Left* and blogger at *The God Article* on Patheos

A Woman Called God presents a fun and "just as logical" alternative to the traditional and patriarchal male God. Yet simmering beneath the playful surface are serious questions: If God had been thought of as a woman for these thousands of years, would women and girls today be hidden in burkas, raped on streets or on campuses, or stolen from schools and sold into sexual slavery? And would men suffer the frustration, anger, fear, and sense of enormous inadequacy when they find it impossible to live up to this artificial pinnacle of power and perfection "in whose image they were made"?

Follow us on Facebook

Second Edition available on Amazon in paperback and Kindle editions. Proceeds from the sale of this edition go to fight violence against women throughout the world.
A Little books for Big people™ publication